Above: George W. Bush's Grandfather Prescott Bush raised $50 million on Wall Street for Hitler and the Nazis. photo: SANDRA BAKER/LIAISON AGENCY 1941 **Below:** Hitler was called the "The Miracle of the 20th Century" by General Motors, and was supported by Ford, Chase Manhattan, and DuPont for his union-bashing and pro-business policies. photo: HULTON-GETTY/LIAISON AGENCY 1933

ABOVE: The U.S.S. California burns off Oahu Island, December 7, 1941. The U.S. was drawn into the following the surprise attack at Pearl Harbor. *But was it a surprise?*

SAVING PRIVATE POWER:

THE HIDDEN HISTORY OF "THE GOOD WAR"

MICHAEL ZEZIMA
AKA
MICKEY Z

AMERICAN SPORTS HERO JESSE OWENS won four gold medals at the Berlin Olympics, effectively disproving fascism in a single bound. Hitler refused to shake his hand. HULTON GETTY/LIAISON AGENCY 1941.

"THE MOST VISIBLE PRO-NAZI/ANTI-COMMUNIST AMERICAN ISOLATIONIST," Colonel Charles A. Lindbergh, Jr. inspected Hitler's air force and concluded Adolf was "undoubtedly a great man." He returned to the States and urged the nation not to go to war against the Third Reich. AP/WIDE WORLD PHOTOS

The Soviet Army and undercover Soviet citizen "partisans" turned back the Nazi invasion at Stalingrad (ABOVE). Male and female, young and old built a Soviet guerrilla resistance to the Nazi occupation. Their victories at Moscow and Stalingrad inspired fierce resistance to the Nazis in Western Europe, for they showed that Hitler was not unbeatable. HULTON GETTY/LIAISON AGENCY 1941.

CLASS WAR: World War I Veterans form the "Bonus Army" and march on Washington, asking for early payment of their bonus pay. President Hoover labeled them "Red agitators," and MacArthur's calvary trampled, bayonetted and burnt out their camp. The Great Depression ended thanks only to the increased demands of wartime production.
AP/WIDE WORLD PHOTOS.

Advertising expertise was recruited by the US Department of War Information to effectively sell the war. **LEFT:** Early efforts failed to relate to factory workers, who felt "HE'S WATCHING YOU" referred to "the boss." **BELOW:** Marketing Research showed that most people thought this poster depicted a soldier and a mobster, not a riveter.

BELOW, LEFT: Advertising mogul George Gallup soon concluded that the campaign had to appeal and be understood by the "lower third" of the population, and "appeal to the emotions."
BELOW, RIGHT: Management competed with unions to display maximum patriotism.

ABOVE: With his newspaper *Social Justice* and a radio show with 20-40 million listeners, Father Coughlin's anti-communist and anti-Jewish vitriol called for isolationism and support for Germany. The Nazi press called him "America's most powerful radio commentator."

BELOW: A storefront in present-day Queens, New York claims to have "no regrets" about bombing Japan. But Secretary of War Henry Stimson himself noted "...There had been no protest over the air strikes we were conducting against Japan which led to such extraordinarily heavy loss of life...there was something wrong with a country where no one questioned that."

To My Parents

*Thanks for a lifetime of unconditional love
and support, and for encouraging me to maintain
an independent mind—even if it meant we'd disagree.*

"We just love the myths we live by. To uncover a truth of the past, a harsh truth, is very hard. It's much easier not to. In America, we have something over and beyond denial. I call it erasure of the past. We're suffering from a national Alzheimer's disease. It's sort of a self-imposed amnesia."

—*Studs Terkel*

CONTENTS

Saving Private Power:
The Hidden History of "The Good War"
by Mickey Z
a.k.a. Michael Zezima
© 2000 Michael Zezima
isbn 1-887-128-45-X

Front Cover Art: Seth Tobocman
Author Photos: Damian Achilles
Art Direction and Design: Sander Hicks
Editorial: Sander Hicks & Nick Mamatas

SPECIAL THANKS:
Richard Derus and CMLA
Bill Koehnlein,
Liaison Photo Agency,
Princeton Architectural Press and Caroline Green
Marilyn Rader &
Howard Zinn.

FIRST EDITION April, 2000
Soft Skull Press, Inc.
Vanguard Press of the Lower East Side
100 Suffolk Street
NYC, USA

WWW.SOFTSKULL.COM

PREFACE
x x x

"Fortunately, we were on the winning side..."

conversation about a movie set this book in motion. Two people, one a Vietnam vet, were discussing the 1998 film *Saving Private Ryan.*
Yes, both agreed, war is "really like that opening sequence."

"You know," the vet confided, "I saw my share of it in 'Nam."

When it came time to question the motives of those who sent "our boys" to face such carnage, even the vet had to admit that little about the Vietnam War could justify this action.

"But," he hastily added, "World War II was different. That was a just war."

Was WWII a just war? Is the "Good War" fable rooted in reality, false hope, or propaganda? This enduring myth goes well beyond Memorial Day barbecues and flickering black-and-white movies on late night TV. WWII is the most popular war in American history: 18 million served in the armed forces while 25 million home-front workers gave regularly to war bonds[1]. According to the accepted history, it was an inevitable war forced upon a peaceful people thanks to a surprise attack by a sneaky enemy. This war, then and now, has been carefully and consciously sold to us as a life-and-death battle against pure evil. For most Americans, WWII was nothing less than good and bad going toe-to-toe in khaki fatigues.

But, Hollywood aside, John Wayne never set foot on Iwo Jima. Despite the former president's dim recollections, Ronald Reagan did not liberate any concentration camps. And, contrary to popular belief, FDR never actually got around to sending American troops "over there" to take on Hitler's Germany until after the Nazis had already declared war on the U.S.

American lives weren't sacrificed in a holy war to avenge Pearl Harbor nor to end the Nazi Holocaust, just as the Civil War wasn't fought to end slavery. WWII was about territory, power, control, money, and imperialism. Sure, the Allies won and ultimately, that's a very good thing—but it doesn't mean they did it fair and square. Precisely how unfairly they behaved will be explored in detail herein but, for now, the words of U.S. General Curtis LeMay, commander of the 1945 Tokyo fire bombing operation, will suffice: "I suppose if I had lost the war, I would have been tried as a war criminal. Fortunately, we were on the winning side."[2]

Not everyone was oblivious to the true motives behind WWII. In a 1939 satirical skit, for example, the Communist Party, USA lampooned the media-created image of a noble war.

"We, the governments of Great Britain and the United States," the skit writers proclaimed, "in the name of India, Burma, Malaya, Australia, British East Africa, British Guyana, Hong Kong, Siam, Singapore, Egypt, Palestine, Canada, New Zealand, Northern Ireland, Scotland, Wales, as well as Puerto Rico, Guam, the Philippines, Hawaii, Alaska, and the Virgin Islands, hereby declare that this is not an imperialist war."[3] Journalist Paul Mattick offered a more straightforward critique of WWII:

> If all the other issues of this war are still clouded, it is perfectly clear that this war is a struggle between the great imperialist contestants for the biggest share of the yields of world production, and thus for the control over the greatest number of workers, the richest resources of raw material and the most important industries. Because so much of the world is already controlled by the small competitive power groups fighting for supreme rule, all controlled groups in all nations are drawn into the struggle. Since nobody dares to state the issues at stake, false arguments are invented to excite the population to murder. The powerlessness of the masses explains the power of current ideologies.[4]

These "false arguments" had enormous influence. Even much of the American left were eventually taken under their sway. When Nazi Germany invaded Soviet Russia in 1941, as historian Howard Zinn documents, "the American Communist party, which had repeatedly described the war between the Axis Powers and the Allied Powers as an imperialist war, now called it a 'people's war' against Fascism."[5]

To begin the process of comprehending some of the myths and false arguments surrounding this so-called people's war, it is instructive to examine what is currently being taught and written on the subject. To do that, throughout *Saving Private Power*, I will refer to some popular mainstream books along with a specific college-level history textbook now in use: *Western Civilization: A Brief History* [6] (a title that cannot help but evoke Gandhi's reply to the query, "What do you think of Western civilization?" He said, "I think it would be a very good idea.").

The selection of this particular book is obviously not meant to represent the contents of all college-level history texts. Rather, it was chosen for its distinct "average-ness." Specifics may vary from text to text, but the main thrust of what is being conveyed about WWII remains intact—thanks not only to school books, but mainstream commentators like Stephen Ambrose, Tom Brokaw, and Colin Powell.[7]

Both volumes of the third edition of *Western Civilization* were updated in 1997 by author Marvin Perry of Baruch College, City University of New York. In his preface, Perry tells us that "Western civilization is a grand but tragic drama," and warns us that he "has been careful to avoid superficial generalizations that oversimplify historical events."

In the second volume (starting with the 1400s), Perry dedicates two chapters (a grand but tragic total of 63 pages) to WWII and the events he claims led up to it, but remarkably offers no index entry for "war crimes." (He *did* call it a "brief" history.) The author remains diligent in his guard against "superficial generalization" as he starts the chapter on WWII by declaring that "...few [historians] would deny that World War II was Hitler's war."

It is precisely that brand of oversimplification that, I feel, makes *Saving Private Power* necessary. We can not afford to chalk up all global violence to a select few inhuman enemies of the United States, who act out their villain's role in some grand but tragic drama. In a nation like ours, with a defense budget of over $250 billion per year, we are *all* partially responsible for every car bomb, every land mine, and every sanctions-related death—even those who choose to fight against it. Entire wars cannot and must not be foisted upon one man.

Nazi propagandist Joseph Goebbels once said, "It is not enough to reconcile people more or less to our regime, to move them towards a position of neutrality towards us, we want rather to work on people until they are addicted to us."

Thus, it is our moral obligation to see through our own propaganda and kick the addictive habit of lazy thinking. Our duty is to discover, for example, what is *not* shown in films like *Saving Private Ryan*—e.g. the crucial fact that by the time of the D-Day invasion, the Russians were engaging 80 percent of the German Army.

"As regards the defeat of Hitler, D-Day itself, was, relatively speaking, and not to downgrade heroism and sacrifice, a sideshow," remarks journalist Alexander Cockburn. "The war had already been won on the Eastern front by the Russians at Stalingrad and then, a year before D-Day, at the Kursk Salient, where 100 German divisions were mangled. Compared with those epic struggles, D-Day was a skirmish.... Hitler's generals knew the war was lost, and the task was to keep the meeting point between the invading Russians and Western armies as far east as possible."[8]

Saving Private Power will address these and many other uncomfortable truths about WWII while focusing on the public relations and media propaganda used by Western corporate states to transform a conflict between capitalist nations into a holy crusade.

❂

What I experienced from viewing *Saving Private Ryan* was a feeling of dread and guilt. I knew as I sat in that comfortable, air-conditioned theater, watching the scenes of bloody warfare unfold, that bombs were exploding in many places across the globe. Machine guns were being fired on soldiers and civilians and activists and dissidents. Land mines were blowing off legs without any concern for ideology. And not only were many of these weapons produced thanks to American taxpayers like me, the death and destruction was being justified by someone somewhere as being part of a good cause.

I was moved then to do my part to help peel away the layer of propaganda that obscures the imperialist motives of most military conflicts, turning them instead into patriotic exercises with all the pathos of a video game. Addressing each war was not an option. Analyzing every economic factor and ideology was not my goal. My goal, as stated here, was to challenge the "Good War" myth: how it came to be, who perpetrated it, who benefits from it, and what is its legacy.

My hope is that by exposing the lie of such a powerful and enduring myth, we can all begin questioning everything being marketed to us within our commodity culture. *Saving Private Ryan*, by bringing home the insanity and suffering of warfare, has led directly to *Saving Private Power* which, I feel, can help explain how that insanity and suffering has been packaged and sold as inevitable and necessary... and good.

For me, the main difference between WWII and any other bloody military conflict throughout history is scope: with high-end estimates of 50 million dead bodies scattered across the entire globe from Nanking to Dresden, from Hiroshima to Auschwitz, from Pearl Harbor to Stalingrad. Our debt to those 50 million is to not glorify or romanticize their deaths; instead we must struggle to comprehend the truths behind the facade and analyze the motivations of the nations involved.

Finally, I must address some of the questions *Saving Private Power* will undoubtedly provoke. Again, of course I think it's good that Hitler was defeated. This book is not meant to defend the Axis powers in any way. Rather, what must be addressed is the reality that having whipped the forces of evil in a noble and popular war, the United States and many of its allies—despite committing their own atrocities during WWII—can now wave the banner of humanitarianism and intervene with impunity across the globe without their motivations being questioned. Especially when every enemy of the U.S. is likened to Hitler.

As for whether or not the U.S. should have entered the war, there are many "if onlys" to consider before answering that question. If only the Allies hadn't invaded Russia after World War I or forced the Germans to submit at Versailles or supported the fledgling fascist regimes in Italy and Germany or had chosen negotiation instead of economic warfare in the Pacific. The list goes on. However, since a certain path was taken, a certain answer must be given. Once the U.S. and its allies had made all of the decisions that brought the world closer to war, the military defeat of the Axis became imperative. While it was never a specific goal, the liberating of the death camps was urgent. Even after decades of animosity, relieving the murderous pressure placed on the Soviet people on the Eastern front was critical. In the end, by waging a ruthless imperialist war, the Allies were able to attain their own short-sighted goals while tangentially doing some good.

If we can somehow ignore all the "if onlys," this is at best a fair trade-off, but certainly not a just and noble mission.

World War II was not inevitable and its legacy is far from "good." The U.S. did not join the global fray to liberate the death camps, to end fascism, or to make the world safe for democracy. Until one of its colonies was attacked, America did nothing more than provide aid to Britain while simultaneously trading with Germany, Italy, and Japan. Until Hitler declared war on the U.S., America would not fight Nazi Germany. While WWII can undoubtedly provide many incredible stories of individual heroism, it was never the good war we've been taught it was.

Truths like this may be ugly but that's why the big lies are invented in the first place. As U.S. Attorney General-turned-human rights activist, Ramsey Clark, has warned about examining the behavior of the U.S. capitalist state, "It is hardest for those who want to love their country and still love justice."(9)

I believe we must first come together to work for and *achieve* justice before we can ever dream of living in a country worth loving.

BY THE NUMBERS

While the precise number of deaths caused by the "Good War" will never be known, the following list provides a sobering place to start counting[10]:

- Australia: 26, 976
- Austria: 280,000
- Belarus ("White Russians"): more than 2,000,000 (25 percent of the population; 25 percent of which were POWs)
- Canada: 32,714
- China: 1,324,516
- France: 201,568
- Germany: 3,250,000
- Roma: roughly 300,000 (one-third of Europe's Roma population)
- Hungary: 147,435
- India: 32,121
- Italy: 149, 496
- Japan: 1,270,000
- Jews: roughly 6,000,000
- New Zealand: 11,625
- Poland: 3,000,000 (20 percent of the population)
- Soviet Union: (battle deaths) 6,115,000
- Ukraine: 4,000,000 to 5,000,000 (1,000,000 were soldiers captured by Germans who then died in prison)
- United Kingdom: 357,116
- United States: (battle deaths) 292,171 (Army: 234,874; Navy: 36,950; Marines: 19,773; Coast Guard: 574). Total deaths: 405, 399. Total casualties: 1,078,162
- All others (Southeast Asians, Burmese, Filipinos, etc.): never calculated with any accuracy.

NOTES FOR PREFACE

1. Howard Zinn. *A People's History of the United States* (New York: HarperPerennial, 1995) p. 398

2. It is useful to note LeMay's later role as U.S. Air Force chief of staff from 1961 to 1965 when he immortalized himself by declaring his desire to "bomb [the North Vietnamese] back into the Stone Age." LeMay also served as vice presidential candidate on George Wallace's 1968 ticket.

3. Zinn, p. 398

4. From the Fall 1941 issue of *Living Marxism*, quoted by Robert F. Barsky in *Noam Chomsky: A Life of Dissent* (Cambridge, MA: The MIT Press, 1997) p. 39

5. Zinn, p. 398

6. *Western Civilization: A Brief History, Volume II, From the 1400s* (Boston: Houghton Mifflin Company, 1997) is used in approximately 130 schools nationwide, and the publisher characterizes it as being "very well-received and respected" and "one of the best selling brief history texts," written by a "well-respected scholar."

7. For an example of such mainstream commentary, consider Colin Powell's description of the term "G.I." in *Time* (June 14, 1999, pp. 71-3): "...two generations later [it] continues to conjure up the warmest and proudest memories of a noble war that pitted pure good against pure evil—and good triumphed.... They were truly a 'people's army,' going forth on a crusade to save democracy and freedom, to defeat tyrants, to save oppressed peoples and to make their families proud of them.... for most of those G.I.s, World War II was the adventure of their lifetime. Nothing they would ever do in the future would match their experiences as the warriors of democracy, saving the world from its own insanity."

8. Alexander Cockburn. *The Golden Age Is in Us* (New York: Verso, 1995) p. 400

9. Ramsey Clark. *The Fire This Time: U.S. War Crimes in the Gulf* (New York: Thunder's Mouth Press, 1992) p. xviii

10. Sources: *The 1999 World Almanac and Book of Facts* (Mahwah, NJ: World Almanac Books, 1999) and *Rand McNally Historical Atlas of the World* (Skokie, IL: Rand McNally, 1991)

CHAPTER ONE

"Keep 'em Smiling..."

1942, US TREASURY DEPT.

"Every government is run by liars
and nothing they say should be believed."

—I. F. Stone

pon discovering some of the less familiar and less favorable aspects of World War II discussed in this book, it is only natural to ponder the method by which these details have managed to slip through the proverbial cracks.

That method, of course, is propaganda. Call it public relations, call it spin, or call it hype, but the truth does not change. It's propaganda.

The same method that served Goebbels.

It is the same method that long ago substituted celluloid images of virile white male millionaires—looking heroic as they conquered one Pacific island after another—in place of the cynical, confused, sometimes-frightened/sometimes-brave cannon fodder who simply followed orders. The real-life human combatants who just attempted to survive in decidedly un-Hollywood scenarios like those at Okinawa have a different story to tell. Ex-Marine E.B. Sledge, for example, gives us a glimpse of reality:

> ...The worst was a week-long stay in rain-soaked foxholes on a muddy ridge facing the Japanese, a site strewn with decomposing corpses turning various colors, nauseating with the stench of death.... Because there were no latrines and because there was no moving in daylight, the men

relieved themselves in their holes and flung the excrement out into the already foul mud.... . If a Marine slipped and slid down the back slope of the muddy ridge, he was apt to reach the bottom vomiting. I saw more than one man lose his footing and slip and slide all the way to the bottom only to stand up horror-stricken as he watched in disbelief while fat maggots tumbled out of his muddy dungaree pockets, cartridge belt, legging lacings, and the like. It is too preposterous to think that men could actually live and fight for days and nights on end under such terrible conditions and not be driven insane.... To me, the war was insanity."[1]

Thanks to a well-oiled public relations machine, WWII was not "insanity" for you and I. It was "good."

DON'T WORRY, BE HAPPY

When the U.S. entered WWII, patriotism was the watchword and denial was the order of the day. For example, the publicity arm of the American Motion Picture Industry put out a full-page ad in several magazines in 1942. Entitled "Our Morale is Mightier than the Sword," the ad declared that in order to win the war, "[o]ur minds must be as keen as our swords, our hearts as strong as our tanks, our spirits as buoyant as our planes. For morale is a mighty force—as vital as the materials of war themselves...so it is the job of the Motion Picture Industry to *keep 'em smiling*." [emphasis in original][2]

Indeed, if the folks back home had any idea what was really going on, few of them would have been *smiling*. That was the true genius of "Good War" propaganda: lies of omission.

Celebrated author John Steinbeck served as a war time correspondent. "We were all part of the war effort," he later remarked. "We went along with it, and not only that, we abetted it.... I don't mean that the correspondents were liars.... It is in the things not

14

mentioned that the untruth lies." Steinbeck went on to explain that "the foolish reporter who broke the rules would not be printed at home and in addition would be put out of the theater by the command."[3]

"By not mentioning a lot of things," adds author Paul Fussell in *Wartime*, "a correspondent could give the audience at home the impression that there were no cowards in the service, no thieves and rapists and looters, no cruel or stupid commanders."[4]

Let's take a look at some of what we weren't told about the "greatest generation," as we just keep *smiling*:

With few exceptions, the Hollywood version of war evokes images of the noble everyman, fighting for freedom and honor without asking any questions. Watching John Wayne or Tom Hanks perform their patriotic duty helps obscure many battlefield realities that would put the "Good War" label in doubt. Some of those realities:

- At least 50 percent of U.S. combat soldiers soiled themselves during battle.
- Ten percent or more of American troops took amphetamines at some time.
- By the war's ends, there were roughly 75,000 U.S. MIAs, most of whom, thanks to modern weaponry, "had been blown into vapor."
- Only 18 percent of combat veterans in the Pacific said they were "usually in good spirits."
- The psychological breakdown rate of men consistently in action for 28 days ran as high as 90 percent.
- As of 1994, roughly 25 percent of the WWII veterans still in the hospital were psychiatric cases.
- About 25 to 30 percent of wartime casualties were psychological cases (under severe conditions, that number could reach 70 to 80 percent).
- Mental problems accounted for 54 percent of total casualties in Italy.
- During the battle for Okinawa, 7,613 Americans died

and 31,807 sustained physical wounds, while an astounding 26,221 were mental casualties.[5]

For those on the homefront, the good old days don't exactly pan out either. Part of the more recent "Good War" facade is the "greatest generation" hype. This fiction enables the family values crowd to claim that generation as their own despite the fact that those who lived during the Depression and WWII were no more or less human than the rest of us. There were a record-high 600,000 divorces in 1946. In addition, the divorce rate in 1940 was 16 percent; by 1944, it had jumped to 27 percent. Between 1939 and 1945, illegitimate births in the U.S. rose by 42 percent. The venereal disease rate for girls 15 to 18 in New York City increased 204 percent between 1941 and 1944, while truancy in Detroit jumped 24 percent between 1938 and 1943.[6]

As for the legendary efficiency of homefront war production, the results are mixed. Despite the fable of unquestioned unity, the forces of labor remained focused on the issue of workplace reform. There were some 14,000 strikes involving nearly seven million workers during the war years. "In 1944 alone," says Zinn, "a million workers were on strike, in the mines, in the steel mills, in the auto and transportation equipment industries."

In those days, WWII poster art was as ubiquitous as labor unrest. Distributed by the U.S. Office of War Information, these colorful single-sheet posters demonized the enemy, canonized "our boys," and helped restore the tattered image of corporate America—all in the name of increasing production, erasing the Depression, and selling the war to a decidedly suspicious public. Representatives from major advertising firm Young & Rubicam, Inc. argued that the "most effective war posters appealed to the emotions," and must be understood by the "lower third" of the population.[7] Battlefield casualty images were banned and any labor-management tensions were glossed over. Thus, the consciously fabricated—but effectively unifying—patriotism of the war effort made it harder for labor to mobilize public support for actions against corporations.

In 1942, when the United Auto Workers (UAW) prepared a poster that trumpeted the auto workers' achievements in the war effort, General Motors rushed out its own advertisement that "undercut the UAW's claim and set in motion the company's wartime public relations campaign."[8]

After the war, the AFL and CIO (both of whom eventually caved in to pressure and issued a no-strike pledge during the war) continued to produce posters in the hope of promoting a more egalitarian social agenda, e.g. national health insurance, higher wages, civil rights, etc. But, organized labor soon fell victim to America's next great public relations campaign: McCarthyism.

WWII poster art also served to define the role of American women in the war effort. "We Can Do It!" said Rosie the Riveter, with "it" meaning following orders on the factory floor until the war was over and then returning to the kitchen.

"This image," says historian Maureen Honey, "both idealized women as a strong, capable fighter infused with a holy spirit and undercut the notion that women deserved and wanted a larger role in public life."[9]

For those working in the shadow of those posters, safety became a major factor. Contrary to the Rosie the Riveter-style propaganda that endures to this day, accidents were common. Under pressure to supply energy for the manufacture of war materials, coal miners, for example, were overworked under often dangerous conditions. Author David Wright has documented some other events that clearly don't fit the fictionalized image of the WWII homefront:

> An ammunition plant in Elwood, Illinois, blew up in 1942, killing 49 people.... [I]n Cleveland, Ohio, [in 1944], a liquid gas tank explosion killed 135 workers.... The worst wartime rail disaster took place near Philadelphia on September 6, 1943, when seventy-nine passengers died in a massive derailment.... [I]n a famous noncombat crash, a

U.S. B-25 bomber ran into the Empire State Building in New York City on July 28, 1945, killing fourteen.[10]

The worst homefront disaster has been largely forgotten. In 1944, in the northern California town of Port Chicago, military cargo ships were being loaded when the bombs exploded, vaporizing the ships along with much of the town and waterfront.

A total of 320 stevedores were killed; 202 were black Navy enlistees. Since no whites shared in the task of loading bombs at Port Chicago, the 258 surviving blacks refused to return to the treacherous task, declaring that they were merely "munitions fodder."

Punishment was swift and severe. Fifty blacks were brought to trial where they were convicted of mutiny and sentenced to 15 years in prison. The remaining 208 were court-martialed and dishonorably discharged. All 258, however, promptly vanished from the official record.[11]

A BRIEF HISTORY

Many of the wartime propaganda tactics utilized during WWII were honed and refined in the first war to end all wars. In what has been called "perhaps the most effective job of large-scale war propaganda which the world has ever witnessed,"[12] the Committee on Public Information, run by veteran newspaperman George Creel, used all available forms of media to promote the noble purpose behind World War I, "to make the world safe for democracy." The Creel Committee (as it came to be known) was the first government agency for outright propaganda in U.S. history; it published 75 million books and pamphlets, had 250 paid employees, and mobilized 75,000 volunteer speakers known as "four minute men," who delivered their pro-war messages in churches, theaters, and other places of civic gatherings. The idea, of course, was to give war a positive spin. For the entire nineteen months America took part in the First World War, the government prohibited publication of any photographs showing dead U.S. soldiers.[13]

But, before any of those invisible Americans could actually get dead, the nation had to be convinced that doing their part in a campaign of organized mass butchery was a good idea. "It is not merely an army that we must train and shape for war," President Woodrow Wilson declared at the time, "it is an entire nation."[14] The age of manipulated public opinion had begun in earnest.

The preparedness campaign to mobilize American public opinion in favor of joining the First World War was loudly supported by the likes of Teddy Roosevelt, along with U.S. Steel and the Rockefellers, all in the name of familiarizing Americans with "the overseas threat."[15] Although Woodrow Wilson won reelection in 1916 on a promise of peace, it wasn't long before he severed diplomatic relations with Germany and proposed arming U.S. merchants ships—even without congressional authority. Upon declaring war on Germany in December 1917, the president proclaimed that "conformity will be the only virtue and any man who refuses to conform will have to pay the penalty."[16]

At the ready to dish out any such penalties were groups like the American Protective League, a nationwide association of 100,000 who, during the war, conducted 40,000 "citizen arrests" of anyone they deemed a subversive. Academia did its part by firing teachers who dared to question the war effort. College professors were dismissed for merely suggesting that both good and bad German people exist, as in any other group

Nicholas Murray Butler was president of Columbia University during the Great War. "I say this with all possible emphasis," he declared, "that there is no place in Columbia University for any person who acts, speaks, or writes treason. This is the last warning to any among us who are not with whole heart, mind, and strength committed to fight with us to make the world safe for democracy." [17]

In time, the masses got the message and reached a fever pitch of so-called patriotism[18]:

- Fourteen states passed laws forbidding the teaching of the German language.
- Iowa and South Dakota outlawed the use of German in public or on the telephone.
- From coast to coast, German-language books were ceremonily burned.
- The Philadelphia Symphony and New York's Metropolitan Opera Company excluded Beethoven, Wagner, and other German composers from their programs.
- German shepherds were renamed Alsatians.
- Sauerkraut became known as "liberty cabbage."
- Even Irish-American newspapers were banned from the mails because Ireland opposed England—one of America's allies—as a matter of principle.

In June 1917, the Espionage Act was passed. It read in part: "Whoever, when the United States is at war, shall willfully cause or attempt to cause insubordination, disloyalty, mutiny, or refusal of duty in the military or naval forces of the United States, shall be punished by a fine of not more than $10,000 or imprisonment of not more than 20 years, or both."

This act cast a wide net and civil liberties were trampled. In Vermont, for example, a minister was sentenced to 15 years in prison for writing a pamphlet, distributed to five persons, in which he claimed that supporting the war was wrong for a Christian.[19]

Perhaps the best-known target of the act was noted Socialist Eugene V. Debs who, after visiting three fellow socialists in a prison in June 1918, spoke out across the street from the jail for two hours. He was arrested and found guilty, but, before sentencing, Debs famously told the judge:

> Your honor, years ago, I recognized my kinship with all living beings, and I made up my mind that I was not one bit better than the meanest on earth. I said then, and I say now, that while there is a lower class, I am in it; while there is a

criminal element, I am of it; while there is a soul in prison, I am not free.[20]

Eugene Debs remained in prison until 1921. Roughly nine hundred others also did time thanks to the Espionage Act, which is still on the books today.

THE MORE THINGS CHANGE...

The twentieth century has been called the century of genocide, but it has also been a century of propaganda (partially to justify all those murders and recast them in a more favorable light). From World War I right up to the recent U.S./NATO bombing of Yugoslavia, little has changed in the way foreign interventions are aggressively sold to a wary public except the technology by which the lies are disseminated.

Writing more than one hundred years ago, anarchist Emma Goldman describes the national mood at the beginning of the Spanish-American War:

America had declared war with Spain. The news was not unexpected. For several months preceding, press and pulpit were filled with the call to arms in defense of the victims of Spanish atrocities in Cuba. I was profoundly in sympathy with the Cubans and Philippine rebels who were striving to throw off the Spanish yoke.... But I had no faith whatever in the patriotic protestations of America as a disinterested and noble agency to help the Cubans. It did not require much political wisdom to see that America's concern was a matter of sugar and had nothing to do with humanitarian feelings. Of course there were plenty of credulous people, not only in the country at large, but even in the liberal ranks, who believed in America's claim.[21]

NOTES FOR CHAPTER ONE

1. Paul Fussell. *Wartime: Understanding and Behavior in the Second World War* (New York: Oxford University Press, 1989) p. 293-4

2. Fussell, p. 152

3. Fussell, pp. 285-6

4. Fussell, p. 285

5. Michael C. C. Adams. *The Best War Ever: America and World War II* (Baltimore and London: The Johns Hopkins University Press, 1994) , pp. 7, 88, 94-5, 104-5, 112, (for all examples)

6. Adams, p. 35

7. William L. Bird, Jr, Harry R. Rubenstein. *Design for Victory: World War II Posters on the American Home Front* (New York: Princeton Architectural Press, 1998), p. 28.

8. Bird and Rubenstein, p. 58

9. Bird and Rubenstein, p. 87

10. David K. Wright. *A Multicultural Portrait of World War II* (New York: Marshall Cavendish, 1994) p. 35

11. Jerome Agel and Walter D. Glanze. *Cleopatra's Nose, The Twinkie Defense & 1500 Other Verbal Shortcuts in Popular Parlance* (New York: Prentice Hall Press, 1990) p. 73

12. John Stauber and Sheldon Rampton. *Toxic Sludge is Good for You! Lies, Damn Lies, and the Public Relations Industry* (Monroe, ME: Common Courage Press, 1995), p. 21

13. Mike Wright. *What They Didn't Teach You About World War II* (Novato, CA: Presidio Press, 1998) p. 147

14. Ralph Raico, *World War I*, audiocassette, Carmichael, 1989

15. Raico, audiocassette

16. Raico, audiocassette

17. Raico, audiocassette

18. Raico, audiocassette (for all examples)

19. Raico, audiocassette

20. Zinn, p. 359

21. Emma Goldman. *Living My Life* (New York: Dover Publications, Inc., 1931, 1970) p. 226

CHAPTER TWO

"The Miracle of the Twentieth Century..."

"We are a people who do not want to keep much of the past in our heads. It is consider unhealthy in America to remember mistakes, neurotic to think about them, psychotic to dwell upon them."

—Lillian Hellman

T o appreciate the enduring power of the "Good War" myth, one has to accept that in order for good to exist, it must stand in contrast to bad. The Second World War provided us with the epitome of bad, Adolf Hitler—a name now synonymous with megalomania, genocide, and evil.

This being the case, it's understandably difficult for many Americans to grasp the concept of their own nation's widespread, overt assistance to the Nazi regime in the decade prior to WWII. Yet the record shows that Hitler and his methods certainly did garner moral, economic, and technical support from the home of the brave right up to America's somewhat reluctant entrance into the European theater and, in some areas, during the war and well beyond V-E Day.

A crucial component of the "Good War" facade is the fable that the forces of freedom were nobly allied against a unique brand of evil fascism. Accordingly, *Western Civilization* author Marvin Perry limited his pre-war commentary mostly to the oft-discussed Western European appeasement. Students using this text will learn how "the British and the French backed down when faced with [Hitler's] violations of the Versailles treaty and threats of war"—a policy that only served to embolden the German dictator. Little is said about the financial ties between the Allies and the Axis nations; there is absolutely no mention of any shared ideology.

In a rare moment of candor, Perry does reveal that even after its invasion of Ethiopia, Mussolini's Italy "continued to receive oil, particularly from American suppliers." However, for Perry (and many other mainstream historians, for that matter) to go any further than this would be tantamount to challenging more than a half-century of denial. Surely, if the fascist war machine could have been slowed or perhaps even stopped well before hostilities commenced, the Allies—especially the U.S.—would have chosen this course. Why then did the United States opt instead to lend its tacit support to genocide?

BETTER DEAD THAN RED

One theory held by serious historians is that the Cold War really started as World War I was ending—precisely when the U.S. sent roughly 13,000 troops to Russia in 1918 after the Bolsheviks made peace with Germany and withdrew from what they saw as an imperialist war. The troops occupied Siberia and Archangel until 1920—ostensibly, at first, to prevent the Germans from seizing war materiel. After incurring thousands of casualties over the course of two years, the U.S. and its allies retreated (except Japan, which fought on until 1922), putting an end to their attempt to "overthrow the Communist regime," as even Perry admits. However, what Perry's text does not provide is context—why the First World War allies were so concerned about the Bolsheviks and their example of anti-capitalist revolution.

Also missing from *Western Civilization* are the revealing words of Winston Churchill, a man directly involved in the Allied invasion of the Soviet Union by Great Britain, the United States, France, Japan, and others. England's Minister for War and Air during the time, Churchill described the mission as seeking to "strangle at its birth" the Bolshevik state. In 1929, he wrote:

> Were [the Allies] at war with Soviet Russia? Certainly not;
> but they shot Soviet Russians at sight. They stood as
> invaders on Russian soil. They armed the enemies of the
> Soviet Government. They blockaded its ports, and sunk its
> battleships. They earnestly desired and schemed its down-
> fall.[1]

Perry also omits a 1920 Department of War report that characterized this intervention as "one of the finest examples in history
of honorable, unselfish dealings."[2] Nowhere in our textbook can a
curious student find the type of obvious anti-Soviet propaganda
dug up by journalist William Blum who, in his book *Killing Hope:
U.S. Military and CIA Interventions since World War II*, proffered
a list of *New York Times* headlines that appeared "by the end of
1919, when the defeat of the Allies and White Army appeared likely." Some examples:

> Dec. 30, 1919: "Reds Seek War With America"
> Jan. 16, 1920: "Britain Facing War With Reds, Calls
> Council In Paris"
> Feb. 7, 1920: "Reds Raising Army To Attack India"
> Feb. 11, 1920: "Fear That Bolsheviki Will Now Invade
> Japanese Territory"

Correspondingly, the tenor of U.S. thinking vis-a-vis the Soviet
Union in the years leading up the WWII can be accurately discerned through the comments of U.S. Ambassador to the Soviet
Union William Bullitt as he left his post in Moscow in 1936.
According to Daniel Yergin, "Bullitt, and apparently some of those
he left behind in the embassy, believed that only Nazi Germany
could stay the advance of Soviet Bolshevism into Europe."[3] This
statement goes a long way in helping explain the Allies' laissez-
faire attitude towards Hitler who himself, in 1937, admitted that
the English follow "the same guidelines as I do, namely, the over-

riding necessity to annihilate Bolshevism."

As a result, fascist atrocities became acceptable in the face of the Bolshevik virus. With revolutions and nationalist movements springing up in China, Ireland, Bavaria, India, and Kenya (to name a few), what's a little reactionary repression when there is communism to fight?

This anti-communist indoctrination of the American people, says Blum, is "imbibed in their mother's milk, pictured in their comic books, spelled out in their school books; their daily paper offers them headlines that tell them all they need to know; ministers find sermons in it, politicians are elected with it, and *Reader's Digest* becomes rich on it."

SLEEPING WITH THE ENEMY

A common misperception is the emergence of globalization and transnational corporations as being a product of the post-Reagan era. However, while so-called trade agreements like NAFTA, GATT, and the WTO may ordain industry with a remarkable measure of sovereignty, the pursuit of profit long ago transcended national borders and loyalty. In the decades before WWII, doing business with Hitler's Germany or Mussolini's Italy (or, as a proxy, Franco's Spain) proved no more unsavory to the captains of industry than bestowing Most Favored Nation status upon post-Cold War China does today. After all, what's a little repression when there's money to be made?

When William E. Dodd, U.S. ambassador to Germany during the 1930s, declared that "a clique of U.S. industrialists is...working closely with the fascist regime[s] in Germany and Italy,"[4] he wasn't kidding.

"Many leaders of Wall Street and of the U.S. foreign policy establishment had maintained close ties with their German counterparts since the 1920s, some having intermarried or shared investments," says investigative reporter Christopher Simpson.

"This went so far in the 1930s as the sale in New York of bonds whose proceeds helped finance the Aryanization of companies and real estate looted from German Jews...U.S. investment in Germany accelerated rapidly after Hitler came to power." Such investment, says Simpson, increased "by some 48.5 percent between 1929 and 1940, while declining sharply everywhere else in continental Europe."[5]

One benefactor of corporate America's largesse was German banker Hermann Abs who was close enough to *der Führer* to receive advance notice that Germany was planning to seize Austria. Tellingly, upon his death, Hermann Abs was judiciously eulogized by the *New York Times* as an "art collector" whose financial career "took off after 1945." The *Times* piece cryptically quoted David Rockefeller as calling Abs "the most important banker of our time."[6]

It wasn't just the Rockefellers who admired Nazi ingenuity. Among the major U.S. corporations who invested in Germany during the 1920s were Ford, General Motors, General Electric, Standard Oil, Texaco, International Harvester, ITT, and IBM—all of whom were more than happy to see the German labor movement and working-class parties smashed. For many of these companies, operations in Germany continued during the war (even if it meant the use of concentration-camp slave labor)[7] with overt U.S. government support.

"Pilots were given instructions not to hit factories in Germany that were owned by U.S. firms," says author Michael Parenti. "Thus Cologne was almost leveled by Allied bombing but its Ford plant, providing military equipment for the Nazi army, was untouched; indeed, German civilians began using the plant as an air raid shelter."[8]

These pre-war business liaisons carried right on over into the post-war tribunals. "The dominant faction of America's establishment had always opposed bringing Germany's elite to trial," Simpson explained.[9]

The Perry textbook neglects such details, but a sampling follows:

- International Telegraph and Telephone (ITT) was founded by Sosthenes Behn, an unabashed supporter of the Führer even as the Luftwaffe was bombing civilians in London. ITT was responsible for creating the Nazi communications system, along with supplying vital parts for German bombs. According to journalist Jonathan Vankin, "Behn allowed his company to cover for Nazi spies in South America, and one of ITT's subsidiaries bought a hefty swath of stock in the airline company that built Nazi bombers."[10]

  Behn himself met with Hitler in 1933 (the first American businessman to do so) and became a double agent of sorts. While reporting on the activities of German companies to the U.S. government, Behn was also contributing money to Heinrich Himmler's Schutzstaffel (SS) and recruiting Nazis onto ITT's board. In 1940, Behn entertained a close friend and high-ranking Nazi, Gerhard Westrick, in the United States to discuss a potential U.S.-German business alliance—precisely as Hitler's blitzkrieg was overrunning most of Europe and Nazi atrocities were becoming known worldwide.

  In early 1946, having relied on the the Dulles brothers in order to survive his open flirtation with Nazi Germany, instead of facing prosecution for treason, Behn ended up collecting $27 million from the U.S. government for "war damages inflicted on its German plants by Allied bombing."[11] He was in the perfect position to lobby President Truman concerning the newly formed Central Intelligence Group (CIG). Meeting with the chair of the Joint Chiefs of Staff, Admiral William D. Leahy, in the White House, Behn, as recorded in Leahy's diary, generously offered for consideration "the possibility of utilizing the service of [ITT's] personnel in American intelligence activities."

- In December 1933, Standard Oil of New York invested one million dollars in Germany for the making of gasoline from soft coal. Undeterred by the well-publicized events of the next decade, Standard Oil also honored its chemical contracts with I.G. Farben—a German chemical cartel that manufactured Zyklon-B, the poison gas used in the Nazi gas chambers—right up until 1942.

- Other companies that traded with the Reich and, in some cases, directly aided the war machine, before and during this time, included the Chase Manhattan Bank, Davis Oil Company, DuPont, Bendix, Sperry Gyroscope, and the aforementioned General Motors. GM top man William Knudsen called Nazi Germany "the miracle of the 20th century.[12]"

- Prescott Bush, father of President George Bush and grandfather of George W. Bush, worked with his father-in-law, George Herbert Walker, in family firm Union Banking Corporation and raised $50 million for the Nazis, by selling German bonds to American investors from 1924 to 1936. The Federal Government shut them down in 1942, under the Trading With the Enemy Act.[13]

- In 1934, United Aircraft sold enough supplies to the German aircraft industry to facilitate the production of roughly one hundred airplanes per month, while the notoriously influential William Randolph Hearst met with Hitler that same year—shortly after the "Night of the Long Knives"[14]—and returned home enthusiastically advocating a peacekeeping alliance between the U.S., Britain, and Germany.

- On the governmental front, U.S. Under Secretary of State Breckinridge Long curiously gave the Ford Motor Company permission to manufacture Nazi tanks while simultaneously restricting aid to German-Jewish refugees because the Neutrality Act of 1935 barred trade with belligerent countries. Miraculously, this embargo did not include petroleum products and Mussolini's Italy tripled its gasoline and oil imports in order to support its war effort while Texaco exploited this convenient loophole to cozy up to Spain's resident fascist, Generalissimo Francisco Franco.

And then there was Sullivan and Cromwell, the most powerful Wall Street law firm of the 1930s. John Foster Dulles and Allen Dulles—the two brothers who guided the firm; the same two brothers who boycotted their own sister's 1932 wedding because the groom was Jewish—served as the contacts for the company responsible for the gas in the Nazi gas chambers, I.G. Farben. During the pre-war period, the elder John Foster led off cables to his German clients with the salutation "Heil Hitler," and he blithely dismissed the Nazi threat in 1935 in a piece he wrote for the *Atlantic Monthly*. In 1939, he told the Economic Club of New York, "We have to welcome and nurture the desire of the New Germany to find for her energies a new outlet."

"Hitler's attacks on the Jews and his growing propensity for territorial expansion seem to have left Dulles unmoved," writes Robert Edward Herzstein. "Twice a year, [Dulles] visited the Berlin office of the firm, located in the luxurious Esplanade Hotel."[15]

Ultimately, it was little brother Allen who actually got to meet the German dictator, and eventually smoothed over the blatant Nazi ties of ITT's Sosthenes Behn.

"(Allen) Dulles was an originator of the idea that multinational corporations are instruments of U.S. foreign policy and therefore exempt from domestic laws," Jonathan Vankin writes. This idea later took root in U.S.-dominated institutions like the World Bank, International Monetary Fund, and World Trade Organization.

Leonard Mosley, biographer of the Dulles brothers, defends Allen by evoking the never-fail, all-purpose alibi of anti-communism. The younger Dulles, Mosley claims, "made his loathing of the Nazis plain, years before World War II...(it was) the Russians (who tried) to link his name with bankers who financed Hitler." However, in 1946, both brothers would play a major role in the founding of the United States' intelligence community and the subsequent recruiting of Nazi war criminals.

One Third Reich supporter who never required a disclaimer was

Henry Ford, the autocratic magnate who despised unions, tyrannized workers, and fired any employee caught driving a competitor's model. Ford, an outspoken anti-Semite, believed that Jews corrupted gentiles with "syphilis, Hollywood, gambling, and jazz."[16] In 1918, he bought and ran a newspaper, *The Dearborn Independent*, that became an anti-Jewish forum.

The May 22, 1920, *Dearborn Independent* headline blared, "The International Jew: The World's Problem," and thus began a series of ninety-two articles, including "The Jewish Associates of Benedict Arnold" and "The Gentle Art of Changing Jewish Names." By 1923, the *Independent*'s national circulation reached 500,000. Reprints of the articles were soon published in a four-volume set called *The International Jew*, which was translated into sixteen different languages.

"The *New York Times* reported in 1922 that there was a widespread rumor circulating in Berlin claiming that Henry Ford was financing Adolf Hitler's nationalist and anti-Semitic movement in Munich," write James and Suzanne Pool in their book *Who Financed Hitler*. "Novelist Upton Sinclair wrote in *The Flivver King*, a book about Ford, that the Nazis got forty thousand dollars from Ford to reprint anti-Jewish pamphlets in German translations, and that an additional $300,000 was later sent to Hitler through a grandson of the ex-Kaiser who acted as intermediary.[17]"

"Ford's pro-Nazi sentiments reached beyond his pocketbook," writes Doares. "His plants in Germany adopted an 'Aryan-only' hiring policy in 1935, before Nazi law required it." A year later, Ford fired Erich Diestel, manager of the automobile company's German plants, simply because he had a Jewish ancestor.

An appreciative Adolf Hitler kept a large picture of the automobile pioneer besides his desk, explaining that "[w]e look to Heinrich [sic] Ford as the leader of the growing Fascist movement in America." According to Vankin, Hitler hoped to support such a movement by offering "to import some shock troops to the U.S. to help [Ford] run for president."

In 1938, on Henry Ford's 75th birthday, he was awarded the Grand Cross of the Supreme Order of the German Eagle from the

Führer himself. He was the first American (GM's James Mooney would be second) and only the fourth person in the world to receive the highest decoration that could be given to any non-German citizen. An earlier honoree was none other than kindred spirit, Benito Mussolini.

Another well-known American millionaire who, while he may not have contributed directly to the Nazi coffers, did his part to keep his country's military might out of Hitler's way was Joseph P. Kennedy, U.S. Ambassador to Britain during the build-up to WWII.

"I can't for the life of me understand why anybody would want to go to war to save the Czechs," he proclaimed in late 1939, adding, "I have four boys and I don't want them to be killed in a foreign war."

Ironically, while Kennedy did lose his eldest boy in that "foreign war," the global conflict also provided the PT 109 myth that helped catapult another son into the White House.

Economic cooperation with the Axis powers was not limited to the European theater. Writing in *The Nation* on March 1, 1941, I. F. Stone reported that, "During the week ending February 15 [1941] we sent Japan 147,044 barrels of crude oil and 137,657 barrels of lubricating oils. We sent Britain 60,000 barrels of crude and 168,986 barrels of fuel oil the same week. Oil is still neutral."

A cursory glance at the record shows that these numbers were indeed consistent with the previous four years. In 1937, according to Stone, the total value of U.S. petroleum exports to Japan was $43,733,000. In 1938, it was $51,191,000; 1939 was $45,285,000; and for 1940 it jumped to $53,133,000. Eventually, the Commerce Department found such figures embarrassing enough to employ the Orwellian tactic of changing the name "aviation gas" to "high-grade motor fuel in bulk or containers."

SYMPATHY FOR THE DEVIL

A February 20, 1939 rally drew 22,000 avid followers—all marching and raising their arms in a Nazi salute to their leader.
Somewhere near Nuremberg, perhaps? Guess again. The venue was
Madison Square Garden where frenzied members of the German-
American Bund cheered Fritz Kuhn as he stood before a 30-foot
high portrait of George Washington flanked by black swastikas,
leading them in a chant of "Free Amerika!" (a rallying cry which
had just recently replaced "Sieg Heil!"), while thirteen hundred
New York City policemen stood guard outside the building.

A U.S. citizen who served in the German Army during the First
World War, Kuhn's physical appearance has been likened to one of
the characters from the Katzenjammer Kids comic strip. His love
of drink, food, and women other than his wife was surpassed only
by his loyalty to Adolf Hitler and hatred of Jews (like Henry Ford,
he went as far as blaming the Jews for Benedict Arnold's treason).
When asked if there were any good Jews, Kuhn replied, "If a mosquito is on your arm, you don't ask is it a good or a bad mosquito.
You just brush it off."

Capitalizing on the widespread anti-Semitism in 1930s
America, Kuhn stirred up his mostly German-American conscripts
by explaining that Lenin was a Jew, J. P. Morgan had Jewish
blood, and Franklin Delano Roosevelt's real name was
"Rosenfeld." Other anti-FDR rumors spread by his adversaries
were often aimed at the high-profile First Lady, Eleanor, i.e. she
had given the president gonorrhea (which she had "contracted
from a Negro") and she was known to visit Moscow "to learn
unspeakable sexual practices."[18]

Kuhn's endless proselytizing did not go unnoticed by the Third
Reich; he attended the 1936 Olympics as an honored guest and
met Adolf Hitler by special invitation.

"Fritz Kuhn awkwardly presented the Führer with three thousand dollars, a gift for a Nazi relief fund," writes Herzstein. "Hitler was not particularly impressed with this rag-tag group, but this did not bother Kuhn, if he realized at all. Eager to trade on his new notoriety, Kuhn implied that he came home from Berlin bearing Hitler's blessing."

Kindred spirits included the National Gentile League and the Christian Mobilizers whose founder, Joseph E. McWilliams, referred to FDR as "Rosenfeld, the Jew king." Another group, the fascist American Liberty League was subsidized by the DuPont dynasty, explains Bill Doares, as was the "black-hooded, Klan-like Black Legion," an outfit that bombed union halls and murdered blacks, immigrants, and pro-union auto workers in the Midwest. The Rev. Earl Little, Malcolm X's father, was among the Legion's victims.[19]

Then, there was always the Ku Klux Klan itself which enjoyed a revival in the 1920s, reaching five million members and spreading to the North. Virulently racist, anti-union, and anti-communist, the KKK, says T. H. Watkins, "had a profound influence in the Midwest," where "rural fear of urban foreigners" struck "understandable fear into the hearts of African Americans, Jews, Catholics, and anyone else who did not fit the organizations definition of a true American."[20]

During the 1932 presidential campaign, Communist Party candidate William Z. Foster, and his running mate, an African-American named James Ford, incurred the anti-radical wrath of the KKK in Alabama. When Foster was scheduled to appear at a meeting in Birmingham, he received the following telegram from the Klan: YOUR PRESENCE IN BIRMINGHAM ALABAMA SUNDAY OCTOBER 9TH IS NOT WANTED. SEND NIGGER FORD.

Although Foster had already cancelled earlier due to illness, Klansmen set off a smokebomb at the meeting anyway.[21]

Finally, there were the Silver Shirts and their leader, William Dudley Pelley, who came closest to matching Kuhn in popularity and rhetoric. Raving against "wild-haired little kikes [holding] important federal positions," Pelley applied a subtle variation to the FDR "real name" sweepstakes: To the Silver Shirt leader, the president was "Rosenfelt," a Dutch Jew who led the "Great Kosher Administration" and, with the help of Leon Trotsky would transform his country into "the United States of Soviet America" (the always reliable anti-communist rationale yet again).

"Shall the United States go to war at the finagling of a kosher president to make the world safe for Jewish bloodgut?" Pelley asked Americans wary of getting involved in another foreign war. While not nearly as popular as their leader imagined, the Silver Shirts were yet another example of how discontent can lead to scapegoating.

Doing his part to prey on the fears of everyday Americans was Father Charles Coughlin, a Canadian-born Catholic priest who rose to prominence during the Depression as a radio commentator.

"No friend of the Jews, Coughlin believed that Professor Felix Frankfurter and labor leader David Dubinsky exercised undue influence on FDR," says Herzstein. "He called them communists." When Rev. Coughlin was asked by a *Boston Globe* reporter to prove this allegation, the priest belted the journalist in the face.

While his attacks on the Jews did cost him some of his audience, Coughlin remained undeterred in his rantings against the "Christ-killers and Christ-rejecters." He even went as far as reprinting the notorious anti-Semitic tract *Protocols of the Elders of Zion* in his newspaper, *Social Justice*, in 1938. The demagogic clergyman perceived U.S. aid to Britain as the first step in a plan to "substitute Karl Marx for George Washington." For his efforts, the Nazi press labeled Coughlin "America's most powerful radio commentator."

With upwards of fifteen to twenty million listeners (with some estimates as high as forty million) on forty-seven stations, Coughlin's anti-communist, anti-Jewish, and isolationist diatribes found a receptive audience of poor and working-class Americans during the Depression.[22]

It wasn't only the huddled masses who embraced the creeping fascism in Europe. Here is a sampling of the mood among the luckier half:

- Charles R. Crane, a "Park Avenue millionaire with connections that reached the White house," once met with the Nazi dictator, and afterwards said that the U.S. should "let Hitler have his way" with the Jews.[23]

- After a visit to Germany in 1936, film star Mary Pickford declared: "Hitler seems to be a great fellow for the Germans. Things certainly are marvelous now in Germany."[24]

- Novelist Theodore Dreiser proclaimed New York City "a Kyke's dream of a Ghetto." He said, "Hitler was right...the Jews...shouldn't live with others."[25]

- Poet Ezra Pound called Winston Churchill "Weinstein Kirschberg," labeled FDR "Franklin Rosenfeld, the supreme swine and betrayer, who infected the whole State Department with his moral leprosy," and theorized that "if Americans had the sense to abandon Rosenfeld and his Jews, there would never have been a war."[26]

- Representative John E. Rankin of Mississippi blamed America's move towards entering the war on "Wall Street and a little group of our international Jewish brethren." No fan of commentator Walter Winchell, Rankin called the popular columnist "a little slime-mongering kike."[27]

- Senator Burton K. Wheeler of Montana chose a more passive form of complicity. "This talk about Hitler wanting to dominate the world, as he expounded it in *Mein Kampf* doesn't impress me any more than did the boasts of Lenin or Trotsky a few years ago that they were going to make a world revolution. These are fantastic boasts by unpractical egoists.[28]"

With support for fascist ideals running the gamut from Kuhn's rag-tag Nazis and anti-labor southerners in white sheets to bankers, lawyers, writers, and legislators, there was one unifying thread: the always reliable Red Scare. During the Depression, union organizing and economically-motivated uprisings were common enough to strike fear into any capitalist's heart.

At the American Socialist Party convention in 1934, a resolu-tion was adopted declaring the party's opposition to "militarism, imperialism, and war." If war came, the Socialists vowed to organ-ize a "massed war resistance" in the form of a "general strike.[29]"

"Roosevelt's program is the same as that of finance capital the world over," declared Earl Browder, general secretary of the Communist Party of the United States of America (CPUSA), also in 1934. "[I]t is the same as Hitler's plan."[30]

Five years later, Milton Wolff, the national commander of the Veterans of the Abraham Lincoln Brigade, coined the anti-war slo-gan, "The Yanks are not coming."

"Under the dishonest slogan of anti-fascism," said Wolff, "[FDR] prepares the red-baiting, union-busting, alien-hunting, anti-Negro, anti-Semitic Jingoistic road to fascism in America."[31]

Such rhetoric found willing ears among the disenfranchised of the 1930s. By 1934, the CPUSA could claim 25,000 members with another 6,000 in the Young Communist League. More important, however, were the half a million "sympathizers" who found com-mon ground with communists—especially with Browder labeling FDR "more or less a lightning rod for capitalism to protect from danger."[32]

Howard Zinn discusses one group that desperately needed such support:

To white Americans of the thirties…blacks were invisible. Only the radicals made an attempt to break the racial barriers: Socialists, Trotskyists, Communists most of all. The CIO, influenced by the Communists, was organizing blacks in the mass production industries. Blacks were still being used as strikebreakers, but now there were also attempts to bring black and whites together against their common enemy.[33]

This common enemy was quite aware of the potential influence a united working class could wield. "There is a feeling among the masses generally that something is radically wrong," Oklahoma attorney Oscar Ameringer told a House of Representatives subcommittee of the Committee of Labor in 1932. "They are despairing of political action. They say the only thing you do in Washington is to make money from the pockets of the poor and put it into the pockets of the rich. They say that this Government is a conspiracy against the common people."[34]

Perhaps Ameringer's words were inspired by the actions of the Bonus Army. In the spring and summer of 1932, disgruntled, unemployed World War I veterans, government bonus certificates in hand, got the idea to demand payment on the future worth of those certificates (they were issued in 1924, to be paid off in 1945).

Anywhere from 17,000 to 25,000 former doughboys and their families formed a Bonus Expeditionary Force, otherwise known as the "Bonus Army." They marched on Washington and picketed Congress and the president.[35]

Arriving from all over the country, with wives and children or alone, they huddled together, mostly across the Potomac River from the Capitol, in what were called "Hoovervilles," in honor of the president who adamantly refused to hear their pleas. Shacks, tents, and lean-tos sprung up everywhere, and the government and newspapers decided to play the communist trump card for the umpteenth time. Despite the fact that the Bonus Army was made up of 95 percent veterans, the entire group were labeled "Red agitators"—tantamount to declaring open season on an oppressed group of U.S. citizens. Right on cue, Hoover called out the troops which included three soon-to-be heroes.

The commander of the operation was Douglas MacArthur, his young aide was Dwight D. Eisenhower, and the Third Cavalry—which spearheaded the assault—was led by George S. Patton.

The U.S. Army assault on July 28, 1932 included four troops of cavalry, four companies of infantry, a machine gun squadron, and six tanks. After marching up Pennsylvania Avenue, soldiers lobbed tear gas and brandished bayonets as they set fire to some of the tents. In a flash, the whole Bonus Army encampment was ablaze.

"Disregarding orders—a common thread running through his career—MacArthur decided to finish the job by destroying the Bonus Army entirely," historian Kenneth C. Davis writes. "After nightfall, the tanks and cavalry leveled the jumbled camps of tents and packing-crate shacks. It was put to the torch."

MacArthur's efforts took the lives of two veterans and an eleven-week-old baby. In addition, an eight-year-old boy was partially blinded by gas, two police had their skulls fractured, and a thousand veterans suffered gas-related injuries.

After this impressive military success, the members of the Bonus Army were forced to leave Washington and many of them joined the other two million or so Americans who lived their lives on the road during the Great Depression.

"Some states, like California," Davis notes, "posted guards to turn back the poor."

Less than ten years later, MacArthur, Patton, and Eisenhower would be earning a place in history books by sending many of those same disenfranchised poor to grisly deaths on the battlefields of Europe and the Pacific. In 1932, however, lacking the intoxicating allure of patriotism as a tool, those in control of America's capitalist economy had to find another way of dealing with such unrest. This is where the roots of fascist support lay. From the darkened country roads in the anti-union South to the well-lit corridors of power, the example of Hitler's Germany was seen as the answer to the questions being put forth by the international working class.

THE LONE EAGLE

Perhaps the most visible pro-Nazi/anti-communist American isolationist was Colonel Charles A. Lindbergh, Jr. A folk hero like his partner in servile anti-Semitism Henry Ford, Lucky Lindy followed in the isolationist footsteps of his congressman father, Charles A. Lindbergh, Sr., who, in his book *Why Is Your Country at War?*, railed against America's entry into World War I.[36]

On May 25, 1936, the younger Lindbergh, still wielding an abundance of international clout thanks to his *Spirit of St. Louis* exploits, received an invitation to visit Germany—an invite that came "in the name of General Goering and the German Air Ministry." The offer was accepted and Lindbergh landed in Berlin on July 22 of that same year.

As described by his biographer Wayne S. Cole, Lindbergh used that first visit to inspect "an elite Luftwaffe fighter group, a major German air research institute, and Heinkel and Junkers aircraft factories. He piloted two German planes and inspected others—including the JU-87 Stuka dive bomber that was so terrifyingly effective in ground support operations early in the European war."

After a few weeks of touting German air power, Lucky Lindy was feted by Goering at a luncheon and attended the opening ceremonies of the Berlin Olympic Games. Although he did not get to meet Hitler, the famed aviator, according to Cole, characterized the dictator as "undoubtedly a great man" who had "done much for the German people" and helped to make Germany "in many ways the most interesting nation in the world." Other examples of Lindbergh's ability to assess reality include his impression that Hitler was "especially anxious to maintain a friendly relationship with England" and had no intention "of attacking France for many years to come, if at all." Overall, he found developments in

Germany to be "encouraging...rather than depressing."

On his next excursion to the Fatherland, Lindbergh flew himself and his wife to Munich in October 1937 for more aviation-related meetings. Juxtaposing the "headlines of murder, rape, and divorce on the billboards of London" with the situation in Germany, Cole reports that the Colonel noted "a sense of decency" within the Nazi regime "which in many ways is far ahead of our own."

One year later, the American aviator returned to Berlin to attend a "stag dinner" at the U.S. embassy in honor of himself and Hermann Goering. It was there, on October 18, 1938, that Goering bestowed upon Lindbergh—in the name of *der Führer*—the Service Cross of the Order of the German Eagle with the Star. Despite negative press in the States, Cole writes, Lindy saw "nothing constructive gained by returning decorations which were given in periods of peace and good will." (By 1955, with a full decade to digest the horrors of WWII, Lindbergh still insisted that the medal hadn't ever caused him any worry. He never returned it.)

After a brief flirtation with moving his family to Berlin, Lindbergh spent the next several months touring the continent, urging a policy of peace through negotiation, before returning home on the *Aquitania* on April 8, 1939.

"After pronouncing Germany's military superiority, Lindbergh returned to America to become an outspoken leader of the isolationist 'America First' movement, funded with Ford money, that tried to keep the United States out of World War II," writes historian Kenneth C. Davis. He notes that Lindbergh, in one speech, told American Jews to "shut up" and accused the "Jewish-owned press" of pushing the U.S. into the war.[37]

From September 1939, right up to the Japanese attack on Pearl Harbor more than two years later, "Lindbergh was the most praised, the most criticized, and the most maligned noninterventionist in the United States," says Cole. In fact, even *before* he joined the popular anti-interventionist group, the America First Committee, Colonel Lindbergh had made five nationwide radio broadcasts, addressed two public meetings, published three articles in popular national magazines, and testified before two major legislative committees—all in the name of American isolationism.

Even after the Nazis conquered France in 1940, Lindbergh lectured on, declaring that nothing could come of "shouting names and pointing the finger of blame across the ocean" at Hitler and the Germans. Lindbergh's son, Reeve, recalled a speech in which the elder Lindbergh identified three groups that were pushing the U.S. to enter the war, "the British, the Roosevelt Administration and the Jews."[38]

What, one might have wondered at the time, would be the catalyst to spur the reluctant aviator into war? A hint, says Cole, may lie in his declarations that America's "bond with Europe is a bond of race and not of political ideology," and that "the average intellectual superiority of the white race…is countered by the sensate superiority of the black race." Thus, he added, if the white race were "ever seriously threatened, it may then be time for us to take our part in its protection, to fight side by side with the English, French, and Germans, but not with one against the other for our mutual destruction."

The imperialist in America's favorite pilot was rearing its ugly head. While his public posturing was that of a staunch isolationist, Cole explains that the Colonel believed that the U.S. should construct and maintain air bases "in Newfoundland, Canada, the West Indies, parts of South America, Central America, the Galapagos Islands, the Hawaiian Islands, and Alaska."

In his diaries, Nazi propagandist Joseph Goebbels highly praised Lindbergh on several occasions. Here's a sampling:

April 19, 1941: "Public opinion in the USA is beginning to waver. The Isolationists are very active. Colonel Lindbergh is sticking stubbornly and with great courage to his old opinions. A man of honor!"

April 30, 1941: "Lindbergh has written a really spirited letter to Roosevelt. He is the president's toughest opponent.

He asked us not to give him too much prominence, since this could harm him. We have proceeded accordingly."

June 8, 1941: "These American Jews want war. And when the time comes they will choke on it. Read a brilliant letter from Lindbergh to all Americans. It really tells the Interventionists where to get off. Stylistically magnificent. The man has something."[39]

Lindbergh may have had "something," but it definitely wasn't much in the way of reservations concerning Germany's behavior. The best America's most famous navigator could muster was this tepid disclaimer: "They [the Nazis] undoubtedly have a difficult Jewish problem, but why is it necessary to handle it so unreasonably?"

After the Japanese attack on Pearl Harbor, the Colonel quickly became a target of derision. Popular opinion turned against him, and even FDR confided to his Secretary of the Treasury, Henry Morganthau, Jr., that "If I should die tomorrow, I want you to know this. I am absolutely convinced that Lindbergh is a Nazi."

The "Lindbergh Beacon" that sat atop a Chicago skyscraper was quickly renamed the "Palmolive Beacon," and the Colorado Rockies mountain dubbed "Lindbergh Peak" after his cross-Atlantic flight was judiciously rechristened "Lone Eagle Peak."

However, in the end, the damage Lindbergh did to his image was eventually forgiven thanks to the stories of his combat missions in the Pacific war.

"His heroics kept his reputation intact," says Davis.

Hero, isolationist, Nazi apologist, anti-Semite, a figure of national controversy, and then hero again, Colonel Lindbergh's career trajectory was indeed hard to follow. But perhaps an April 25, 1941 editorial in the *Daily Worker* captured the true essence of his durability when it labeled him "a reactionary imperialist, part and parcel of the same imperialist class which runs the show at Washington; he just happens to have a difference of opinion with them at the moment on how best to go about expanding the American empire, and preparing for war against the Soviet Union."

WHEN IN ROME...

Adolf Hitler and his Nazi regime were not the only recipients of American moral support; there was a particular blacksmith's son who also merited the attention of U.S. businessmen and lawmakers alike.

Benito Mussolini, exploiting the fears of an anti-communist ruling class in Italy, installed himself as head of the single-party fascist state in 1925 after declaring three years earlier that, "[e]ither they will give us the government or we shall take it by descending on Rome." Virulently anti-communist, anti-Semitic, and anti-labor like Hitler, *Il Duce* ("the leader") was prone to pronouncements like this one, quoted by our own Professor Perry: "We stand for a new principle in the world. We stand for the sheer, categorical, definitive antithesis to the world of democracy."

Putting this doctrine into action, Il Duce took aim at Italy's powerful unions. The solution, says Michael Parenti, was to "smash their unions, political organizations, and civil liberties.[40]" This included the destruction of labor halls and the shutting down of opposition newspapers.

"In the name of saving society from the Red Menace," Parenti explains, unions and strikes were outlawed in both Italy and Germany. "Union property and farm collectives were confiscated and handed over to rich private owners." Even child labor was reintroduced in Mussolini's Italy.[41]

Despite—or perhaps because of—the Blackshirts, the terror tactics, the smashing of democratic institutions, and the blatant fascist posturing, Mussolini received some rave reviews on both sides of the Atlantic.

"It is easy to mistake, in times of political turmoil, the words of a disciplinarian for those of a dictator. Mussolini is a severe disciplinarian, but no dictator." wrote *New York Times* senior foreign correspondent, Walter Littlefield, in 1922. Further serving the corporate roots of the U.S. media, Littlefield went on to advise that "if the Italian people are wise, they will accept the Fascismo, and by accepting [they will] gain the power to regulate and control it." [42]

Columnist Alexander Cockburn has documented that six days earlier, an unsigned *Times* editorial observed that "in Italy as everywhere else, the great complaint against democracy is its inefficiency...Dr. Mussolini's experiment will perhaps tells us something more about the possibilities of oligarchic administration."[43]

In January 1927, Winston Churchill wrote to Il Duce, gushing that "if I had been an Italian, I am sure I would have been entirely with you from the beginning to the end of your victorious struggle against the bestial appetites and passions of Leninism." Even after the advent of war, Churchill still found room in his heart for the Italian dictator, explaining to Parliament in 1940 that "I do not deny that he is a very great man but he became a criminal when he attacked England."[44]

Other unabashed apologists for Dr. Mussolini included:

- Richard W. Child, former ambassador to Rome, who stated in 1938 that "it is absurd to say that Italy groans under discipline. Italy chortles with it! It is victor! Time has shown that Mussolini is both wise and humane."

- The House of Morgan, who loaned $100 million to the Italian government in the late 1920s, and then reinvested it in Italy upon its repayment.

- Secretary of the Treasury Andrew Mellon, who, also in the late 1920s, renegotiated the Italian debt to the U.S. on terms more favorable by far than those obtained by Britain, France, or Belgium.

•Governor Philip F. La Follette of Wisconsin (considered presidential timber in the 1930s), who kept an autographed photo of Il Duce on his wall.

• A 1934 Cole Porter song originally contained the lyrics, "You're the tops, you're Mussolini." It was eventually changed to "the Mona Lisa.[45]"

• As late as 1940, 80 percent of the Italian-language dailies in the U.S. were pro-Mussolini.[46]

Support from a "higher source" was provided by the ultraconservative Pope Pius XI who shared Mussolini's Bolshevik paranoia. In exchange for Fascist recognition of the independence of Vatican City, the pope bestowed his blessing upon Il Duce's invasion of Ethiopia and his intervention in the Spanish Civil War. Even after Italy had aligned itself with Nazi Germany, the papacy never broke with either Fascist regime.

Finally, for support from the highest of all sources, there was FDR himself who, well into the 1930s, was "deeply impressed" with Benito Mussolini and referred to the Italian ruler as that "admirable Italian gentleman."[47]

THE BUTLER (ALMOST) DID IT

Despite Roosevelt's positive assessment of the strongman of Italian fascism, there is evidence that some home-grown fascists may have cautiously explored the option of an American coup. In 1934, the DuPonts and the Morgans tried to hire former Marine Gen. Smedley Butler (Ret.) to stage a fascist overthrow of the supposedly liberal Roosevelt administration. Later that year, Butler testified before a congressional committee convened to investigate this possible sedition.

After claiming that Wall Street brokers had offered him millions of dollars to set up a fascist army of half a million, Butler explained that Gerald MacGuire of Grayson Murphy and Company had told him that FDR would remain as a figurehead president. Businessmen and generals would run the country and everything would be legal.

Before passing judgement on the veracity of Butler's claims, consider how the general himself summarized his career before a legionnaires convention in 1931:

> I spent 33 years...being a high-class muscle man for Big Business, for Wall Street and the bankers. In short, I was a racketeer for capitalism....I helped purify Nicaragua for the international banking house of Brown Brothers in 1909-1912. I helped make Mexico and especially Tampico safe for American oil interests in 1916. I brought light to the Dominican Republic for American sugar interests in 1916. I helped make Haiti and Cuba a decent place for the National City [Bank] boys to collect revenue in. I helped in the rape of a half a dozen Central American republics for the benefit of Wall Street.[48]

The alleged coup plan fizzled when Butler told FDR about it, thus presenting the president with a new problem. Fearful of the financial fallout of arresting anyone named Morgan or DuPont, FDR chose instead to leak the news to the press. "Not for the first time or last time in his career, [Roosevelt] was aware that there were powers greater than he in the United States," says author Charles Higham.[49]

Press reports led to the congressional investigation, which delved into the role played in the proposed takeover by General Douglas MacArthur.[50] Thanks to the influence of big business, however, Congress found the task of rooting out fascism among U.S. financiers and corporate heads unnecessary.

"Butler begged the committee to summon the Du Ponts," says Higham, "but the committee declined. Nor would it consent to call anyone from the house of Morgan.[51]"

Thus, while the supposed arsenal of democracy was gearing up to do battle with totalitarianism, the very mechanism of its popular support was under strenuous attack from the economic elites in whose hands the power truly lies.

As a certain admirable Italian gentlemen once declared, "Fascism is corporatism."[52]

Notes, Chapter Two

1. William Blum. *Killing Hope: U.S. Military and CIA Interventions Since World War II* (Monroe, ME: Common Courage Press, 1995) p. 9

2. Blum, p. 10

3. Daniel Yergin. *Shattered Peace: The Origins of the Cold War and the National Security State* (Boston: Houghton Mifflin, 1977) p. 26. Such anti-communist fervor was being stoked back in the States by anti-immigration like the McCarran Act of 1924. In *The Great Depression: America in the 1930s* (Boston: Little, Brown and Company, 1993), historian T.H. Watkins explained that the McCarran Act "severely restricted all future immigration...putting special emphasis on limiting the number of Jews and Poles, Slavs, Russians, Italians, and other insufficiently Anglo-Saxon or Nordic-Protestant types." (p. 33)

4. Charles Higham. *Trading with the Enemy: The Nazi-American Money Plot, 1933-1949* (New York: Barnes & Noble Books, 1983), p. 167

5. Bob Spiegelman, "*LOOT* Interviews Christopher Simpson," *Lies of Our Times* May 1994, pp. 13-18. (*Lies of Our Times* was a monthly journal of media analysis.)

6. Spiegelman, p. 15.

7. Bill Doares. "Corporate America & the Rise of Hitler," *Workers World*, May 4, 1995: p. 11. (*Workers World* is a weekly newspaper published by the Workers World Party in New York.)

8. Michael Parenti. *Blackshirts & Reds: Rational Fascism and the Overthrow of Communism* (San Francisco: City Lights, 1997) p. 19

9. Spiegelman, p. 15.

10. Jonathan Vankin. *Conspiracies, Cover-ups and Crimes* (New York: Paragon House, 1991), p. 245

11. Parenti, p. 19

12. Doares, p. 11

13. Union Banking Corp. was eventually seized under the Trading With The Enemy Act. (Office of Alien Property Custodian, Vesting Order No. 248. The order was signed by Leo T. Crowley, Alien Property Custodian, executed October 20, 1942; F.R. Doc. 42-11568; Filed, November 6, 1942, 11:31 A.M.; 7 Fed. Reg. 9097, Nov. 7, 1942). Also, See *The Secret War Against The Jews: How Western Espionage Betrayed*

The Jewish People by John Loftus and Mark Aarons. New York; St. Martins Press, 1994. Also, for an overview of the Bush family, see the Introduction by Nick Mamatas and Toby Rogers to *Fortunate Son: George W. Bush and the Making of an American President* by J.H. Hatfield (New York, NY: Soft Skull Press, 2000)

14. The "Night of the Long Knives" refers to June 29-30, 1934 purge of the Sturmabteilung (SA) ordered by Adolf Hitler. Led by Ernst Röhm, the SA, also known as storm troopers or Brownshirts, was the military wing of the Nazi party. When Röhm and his allies came into conflict with the German Army, Hitler ordered the SS to kill him and some 400 others in a successful effort to consolidate power. Afterwards, Hitler announced that "everyone must know for all future time" that opponents of his regime faced "certain death." Within weeks, Hindenburg had died and Hitler combined the offices of President and Chancellor and took a personal oath of allegiance from the German Army.

15. Robert Edwin Herzstein, *Roosevelt and Hitler: Prelude to War* (New York: Paragon House, 1989), p. 222

16. Herzstein, p. 162

17. In *The Flivver King*, Upton Sinclair wrote of a worker protest over wages at the River Rouge Ford plant in Dearborn, Michigan, in which Dearborn police and Ford's private security men killed four marchers and injured sixty others. After River Rouge, Sinclair declared that Ford cars only came in one color: "fresh human blood."

18. Kenneth C. Davis. *Don't Know Much About History: Everything You Need to Know about American History but Never Learned* (New York: Avon Books, 1990) p. 283

19. Doares, p. 11

20. T.H. Watkins. *The Great Depression: America in the 1930s* (Boston: Little, Brown and Company, 1993) pp. 15, 33

21. Robin D.G. Kelley. *Hammer and Hoe: Alabama Communists During the Great Depression* (Chapel Hill: University of North Carolina Press, 1990) pp. 31-2

22. Peter Jennings and Todd Brewster. *The Century* (New York: Doubleday, 1998), p. 163.

23. Herzstein, p. 162

24. Herzstein, p. 125

25. Herzstein, pp. 159, 162

26. Herzstein, p. 363

27. Herzstein, p. 258

28. Cole, Wayne S., *Charles A. Lindbergh and the Battle Against American Intervention in World War II* (New York: Harcourt Brace Jovanovich, 1974), p. 137

29. Lawrence S. Wittner. *Rebels Against War: The American Peace Movement, 1933–1983* (Philadelphia: Temple University Press, 1984), p. 8

30. David M. Kennedy. *Freedom From Fear: The America People in Depression and War, 1929-1945* (New York: Oxford University Press, 1999) p. 22

31. Harvey Klehr, John Earl Haynes, Fridrilch Igorevich Firsov. *The Secret World of American Communism* (New Haven: Yale University Press, 1995) p. 268

32. Watkins, p. 225

33. Zinn, p. 396

34. Watkins, p. 76

35. Davis, pp. 274-5 (for all his references to the Bonus Army)

36. Cole, p. 18. All unattributed quotes in the section on Lindbergh are from Cole.

37. Davis, p. 267

38. Reeve Lindbergh wrote about his father in a special edition of *Time* magazine (June 14, 1999) p. 75

39. Taylor, Fred, ed., *The Goebbels Diaries, 1939-1941* (London: H. Hamilton, 1982) pp. 322, 341, 400-1

40. Parenti, pp. 6-7

41. Parenti, pp. 6-7

42. Cockburn, p. 391

43. Cockburn, p. 391

44. Joseph Stromberg, *World War II*, audiocassette, Carmichael, 1989

45. Stromberg, audiocassette

46. Adams, p. 36

47. Richard Shenkman. *Legends, Lies & Cherished Myths of World History* (New York: HarperPerennial, 1994), p. 251

48. Eduardo Galeano. *Open Veins of Latin America: Five Centuries of the Pillage of a Continent* (New York, Monthly Review Press, 1973, 1997) p. 108

49. Higham, pp. 163-4

50. Despite being a West Point classmate of Murphy and an outspoken critic of FDR, Douglas MacArthur

was rejected as the coup general because he was hated by WWI veterans after the Bonus Army debacle.

51. Higham, pp. 163-4. Four years later, Higham explains, the congressional committee published its report for "restricted circulation," declaring that all "pertinent statements made by General Butler" had indeed been verified.

52. Vankin, p. 243

CHAPTER THREE

"Surprise and Pain..."

Opposite: Lt. General Lucian K. Truscott, Jr. commanding general of the Fifth Army in Italy, congratulates members of the 92nd Infantry Division after they threw back a German attack near Viareggio, Italy. However, despite heroism such as this and the valor of the 99th Pursuit Squadron of Black aviators, the U.S. troops were segregated until 1948.

"You're not to be so blind with patriotism that you can't face reality. Wrong is wrong, no matter who does it or says it."

—Malcolm X

If there was ever a litmus test for discerning a good war from a bad war, history provided it during WWII. Indeed, the most frequently evoked after-the-fact rationale for the deadliest war in history being labeled a moral battle was the Allies' supposed aim to stop the Nazi Holocaust.

Hitler's "final solution" took the lives of roughly six million Jews along with millions more Slavs, Eastern Europeans, Roma,[1] homosexuals, labor leaders, and suspected communists. If decency played any role, the U.S. would have taken action against Germany some time during the 1930s. Historian Howard Zinn explains that simply, "the plight of Jews in German-occupied Europe, which many people thought was at the heart of the war against the Axis, was not a concern to Roosevelt...[who] failed to take steps that might have saved thousands of lives. He did not see it as a high priority."

As Benjamin V. Cohen, an advisor to FDR, later commented, "When you are in a dirty war, some will suffer more than others.... Things ought to have been different, but war is different, and we live in an imperfect world."[2]

Swirling around the subject of the Holocaust in our "imperfect world" are many questions. Who knew about Hitler's plan and when? What was done to stop it? Were their complicit roles played by factions within the United States? None of these issues, of course, are touched upon in *Western Civilization*, with Perry opting instead to hide behind a simplistic good-vs.-evil mantra, and spewing forth the following analysis of yet another grand but tragic drama:

> The Holocaust was the grisly fulfillment of Nazi racial theories. Believing that they were cleansing Europe of a lower and dangerous race that threatened the German people, Nazi executioners performed their evil work with dedication and resourcefulness, with precision and moral indifference—a gruesome testament to human irrationality and wickedness.

True to his role as commissar in a system of imposed ignorance, Professor Perry evades the larger issues and instead exploits the genocide as an opportunity to question the values of secular humanism and liberalism: "Written into the history of Western civilization," he concludes, "was an episode that would forever cast doubt on the Enlightenment concepts of human goodness, rationality, and the progress of civilization."

Note the passive tone of the opening part of that declaration. It is as if the way history books are written is a force of nature—something humanity cannot change.

We are long overdue for a closer examination of the Nazi Holocaust and how it fits into the "Good War" fantasy. Ultimately, in order to dissect America's action (and inaction) in the face of the slaughter of millions based mostly on ethnic background, it may prove most helpful to first examine how much was known of the genocide as it occurred and what the racial milieu of the U.S. was at the time.

THE FIRST KITCHEN DEBATE

While volumes have been written to correctly challenge those con-temptible historical criminals who deny the Nazi death camps ever existed, one of the more subtle forms of denial is rarely questioned or even mentioned. This particular negation involves the deep-seated belief that the West was simply not aware of the extent of Nazi Germany's atrocities until the war was nearly over and once they knew the truth, they acted expediently to save lives. To accept this fiction is to not only enable oneself to believe that the inaction of the Allies was due merely to lack of information, but to also dis-regard the role of the *Munich Post*—a newspaper the Führer him-self referred to as the "Poison Kitchen."

"The names of the men who risked their lives to publish the truth about Hitler rarely appear in the histories of that era," writes Ron Rosenbaum in *George* magazine (July 1998). "Their full story has never been told, even in Germany, or perhaps especially in Germany, where it's more comforting for the national self-image to believe that nobody really knew who Hitler was until it was too late, until after 1933, when he had too much power…for anyone to resist."

In a century that has provided us with a corporate-owned media in which the verbatim reprinting of State Department press releases passes for journalism, it is at first rather difficult to con-ceptualize the efforts put forth by the fearless editors of the *Munich Post.* However, beginning in 1921, men like Martin Gruber, Erhard Auer, Edmond Goldschagg, and Julius Zerfass (among others) told it like it was about Adolf Hitler and his hang-ers-on—so much so, says Rosenbaum, that they came close to driving the hyper-sensitive überleader to suicide.

In 1931, Hitler's half-niece, Geli Raubal, was found shot dead with her famous uncle's gun by her side. Despite a hasty autopsy and a convenient verdict of suicide, the *Post* seized this opportunity to raise "questions about the nature of Hitler's personal relationship with his niece, giving voice to long-standing rumors of unnatural sexuality," says Rosenbaum. Many front page details appeared to incriminate the future German dictator.

"The public airing of these devastating insinuations brought Hitler to the brink of taking his own life," Rosenbaum states, citing one account about a fellow Nazi "snatching a gun from his hand before he could pull the trigger." Clearly, the *Munich Post* had Adolf Hitler's attention as they began to change the focus of their inquiries.

What began as a regular series of exposés of lurid sex scandals and investigations of the Nazi party's blatant manipulation of facts—a campaign with partisan roots since the *Post* was founded by the Bavarian Social Democratic Party[3]—soon led to early clues about the grim prospect of mass murder. As early as 1931, several years before men like Dulles and Ford and Lindbergh and Behn gave their very public stamp of approval to the fascist state, the *Munich Post* brought to light the Nazi euphemism for genocide, *Endlösung*.

"More than a year before Hitler came to power," Rosenbaum reveals, "the *Post* reported that it had uncovered a 'secret plan' [that would have] 'worked out special orders for the solution of the Jewish question.' " Here's an excerpt from the Dec. 9, 1931 edition of the *Munich Post* (more than a decade before high-ranking Nazis and SS officers met at the Wannsee Conference to obtain full support for "the final solution"):

> For the final solution of the Jewish question, it is proposed to use Jews in Germany for slave labor or for cultivation of the German swamps administered by a special S.S. division.

While there was no specific mention of mass extermination yet, surely even the most cursory reading of the *Munich Post* in Hitler's early days (or, perhaps, a casual browse through *Mein*

Kampf) should have aroused the concern of any nation or states-man genuinely interested in human rights.

Perhaps, in our imperfect world, the Western industrialists envied the way the Nazis smashed unions, persecuted commu-nists, and promoted the divisive concept of superior and inferior "races."

Perhaps the spectre of prison camps (later dubbed "strategic hamlets") was all too familiar to the supposed good guys. "Britain, during the Boer War (1899-1902), had used such camps to restrain the hostile elements of the South African population. So did Spain and America in the Philippines," writes historian Michael C.C. Adams, noting that such precedents had served as models for the Nazi regime.[4]

In fact, inspiration for Germany's policies, says Ward Churchill, professor in the Center for Studies in Ethnicities and Race in America at the University of Colorado at Boulder, goes back even further. "Hitler took note of the indigenous people of the Americas," says Churchill, "specifically within the area of the United States and Canada, and used the treatment of the native people,…the policies and processes that were imposed upon them, as a model for what he articulated as being…the politics of living space. In essence, Hitler took the notion of a drive from east to west, clearing the land as the invading population went and reset-tling it with Anglo-Saxon stock…as the model by which he drove from west to east into Russia—displacing, relocating, dramatical-ly shifting or liquidating a population to clear the land and replace it with what he called superior breeding stock…. He was very con-scious of the fact that he was basing his policies in the prior expe-riences of the Anglo-American population…in the area north of the Rio Grande river.[5]"

It seems the idea of going to war merely to combat racism didn't exactly appeal to the United States—a deeply polarized society with Japanese-American internment camps and strictly segregated armed forces lurking in its immediate future.

ZOOT SUITS AND PINK BRACELETS

The previous chapter—with Henry Ford, Father Coughlin, Ezra Pound, the Bundists, and far too many others—touched on the depth of America's racism in the pre-war years. As a result, it shouldn't be too difficult to envision a somewhat indifferent U.S. response to the news of German persecution of European Jews. Consider two polls discussed by Robert Edwin Herzstein in his book, *Roosevelt and Hitler: Prelude to War*: a March 1938 survey that showed 41 percent of Americans believed that "Jews have too much power in the United States," and a U.S. Army poll taken as the war was ending, in September 1945, that found an astonishing 22 percent of GIs thought the Nazi treatment of the Jews was justified. Another ten percent labeled themselves "unsure."

The racial climate during the WWII years was one of intolerance even for those who served in battle. During the war, blood plasma collected from black soldiers was separated from white blood plasma to avoid the "mongrolization of the white race."[6] This was done by the Red Cross with the approval of the U.S. government. Ironically, the blood bank system was developed by a black physician, Charles Drew, who was initially put in charge of wartime donations but later fired when he spoke out against blood segregation.

"Was the war being fought to establish that Hitler was wrong in his ideas of white Nordic supremacy over 'inferior' races?" Zinn asks. "The United States' armed forces were segregated by race. When troops were jammed onto the Queen Mary in early 1945 to go to combat duty in the European theater, the blacks were stowed down in the depths of the ship near the engine room, as far as possible from the fresh air of the deck, in a bizarre reminder of the slave voyages of old.[7]"

Even those who survived the fighting in one piece faced "miscegenation laws" that prevented black veterans who had married

whites overseas (or whites who had married Asians) from returning to the U.S. In 1948, 15 states still had such laws on the books.
As for the blacks who served their country at home, the situation
is best summed up by one particular spokesman for a West Coast
aviation plant: "The Negro will be considered only as janitors and
in other similar capacities.... Regardless of their training as aircraft workers, we will not employ them." As Army Chief of Staff
General George C. Marshall once bellowed, "Quit catering to the
negroes' desire for a proportionate share of combat units. Put them
where they will best serve the war effort." This usually meant driving trucks, loading cargo, or working as orderlies and messboys.

Institutional racism did not stand unopposed in the United States.
A. Philip Randolph was head of the Brotherhood of Sleeping Car
Porters, an all-black union. Trained as a Shakespearean actor,
Randolph was a gifted orator who spoke out against U.S. involvement in World War I and later played a major role in fighting discrimination during World War II. After warning FDR that he'd
lead a protest march on Washington, the president issued an executive order on June 25, 1941 that barred discrimination not only in
defense industries but all federal bureaus, too. This order created
the Fair Employment Practices Committee.[8]

 However, it wasn't until after the war that Randolph was able
to persuade President Truman to integrate the armed forces. That
executive order was issued on July 26, 1948.

Blacks were certainly not alone in their persecution; gays also
faced the wrath of an American society hungry for scapegoats.
Indeed, in such a hostile and intolerant environment, should anyone have realistically expected a domestic U.S. movement to protect the doomed homosexuals in Nazi concentration camps?

 Gay men, viewed as a potential poison to the purity of the
Aryan race, were forced to wear pink triangles in Germany as
early as 1935. These men were usually put to the hardest labor and
fed the thinnest rations—often facing ridicule from not only the
prison guards but fellow internees alike. Such treatment was

sometimes carried over after the war. Historians Jerome Agel and Walter D. Glanze tell of one particular "pink triangle" who, "after spending three years in a Nazi camp, was required by the Allies to finish another five years of the Nazi-imposed sentence of eight years for sexual deviance.[9]"

Even those gay men who served in the U.S. armed forces were not exempt from discrimination. "Homosexual veterans were frequently denied benefits under the GI Bill, such as college tuition, home loans, job training, and hospital care," says Adams.

Are we more enlightened with the lessons of the Holocaust before us? Certainly not in Florida's Polk County jail, where male and female gay inmates were forced to wear pink bracelets for fifteen years until the ACLU finally challenged this practice in 1989.

Further evidence of the American racial mood in the 1940s were the "Zoot Suit Riots." During the war years, young Mexican workers entered the country *en masse* in response to a worker shortage on the Pacific coast. In time, some Latino youths formed gangs and dressed almost exclusively in zoot suits. A zoot suit, as Glanze and Agel describe it, is made up of a "very long jacket, flared at the bottom, with exaggeratedly padded, boxy shoulders, and pegged sleeves. The trousers are pleated at the waistline, cut very wide over the hips, and taper to such narrow bottoms that men with big feet have trouble slipping the pants on."

While the zoot suit eventually attained widespread popularity in the mainstream, it also became a pejorative synonym for "Mexican" on the West Coast as whites took umbrage at so many able-bodied young men who were not helping to win the war. To the local white population of Los Angeles, the manufacture of the zoot suit was a glaring example of waste in a time that demanded sacrifice in the name of defending democracy. This inevitably led to racist violence sparked by angry white soldiers on leave.

"In June 1943, the 'zoot suit' riots exploded in Los Angeles," Adams says. "For almost a week, off-duty white enlisted personnel roamed the streets, assaulting Hispanics.[10]"

Mexicans and blacks "were dragged into the streets by soldiers and civilians," wrote Agel and Glanze, where they were "stripped and beaten." The response of the Los Angeles city council was predictable and familiar. Rather than address the issues of cheap labor and racism, they made it a misdemeanor to wear a zoot suit. [11]

Added to the hit list of blacks, gays, and Mexicans was one group for whom discrimination was officially legislated: the Japanese. As the next chapter will describe this shameful episode in much greater detail, it is instructive when contemplating the U.S. nonresponse to the Holocaust to reflect upon the words of Japanese-American Hatsuye Egami, a former prisoner of an American internment camp. The imagery speaks volumes in any discussion concerning the U.S. response to Nazi concentration camps:

> Since yesterday, we Japanese have ceased to be human beings. We are numbers. We are no longer Egamis, but the number 23324. A tag with that number is on every trunk, suitcase, and bag. Tags, also, on our breasts.[12]

Another grand but tragic drama in an imperfect world.

ACCESSORIES TO THE CRIME

Apologists can pretend that the details of the Holocaust were not known and if they had been, the U.S. would have intervened, but as Kenneth C. Davis explains, "Prior to the American entry into the war, the Nazi treatment of Jews evoked little more than a weak diplomatic condemnation. It is clear that Roosevelt knew about the treatment of the Jews in Germany and elsewhere in Europe, and about the methodical, systematic destruction of the Jews during the Holocaust. Clearly, saving the Jews and other groups that Hitler was destroying en masse was not a critical issue for American war planners.[13]"

Indeed, when a resolution was introduced in January 1934 asking the Senate and the President to express "surprise and pain" at the German treatment of the Jews, the resolution never got out of committee.

Such inaction was not reversed even as more specific details began to reach the average American. On October 30, 1939, the *New York Times* wrote of "freight cars...full of people" heading eastward and broached the subject of the "complete elimination of the Jews from European life" which, according to the *Times*, appeared to be "a fixed German policy.[14]"

As for the particulars on the Nazi final solution, as early as July 1941, the New York Yiddish dailies offered stories of Jews massacred by Germans in Russia. Three months later, the *New York Times* wrote of eyewitness accounts of ten to fifteen thousand Jews slaughtered in Galicia. On December 7, 1942, the *London Times* joined the chorus with this observation:

> The question now arises whether the Allied Governments, even now, can do anything to prevent Hitler's threat of extermination from being literally carried out.[15]

The German persecution and mass murder of Eastern European Jews was indeed a poorly kept secret and the United States and its Allies cannot honestly nor realistically hide behind the excuse of ignorance.

Even when the Nazis themselves initiated proposals to ship Jews from both Germany and Czechoslovakia to Western countries (or even Palestine) the Allied nations could never get beyond negotiations and the rescue plans never materialized.

One particularly egregious example was the 1939 journey of the *St. Louis*. Carrying 1,128 German Jewish refugees from Europe, the ocean liner was turned back by U.S. officials because the German immigration quota had been met. The *St. Louis* then returned to Europe where the refugees found temporary sanctuary in France, Great Britain, Belgium, and the Netherlands. "Most the emigrees were eventually captured by the Nazis after their invasion of the Low Countries in the spring of 1940 and were shipped to death camps," wrote Agel and Glanze.[16]

Haskel Lookstein, author of *Were We Our Brothers' Keepers?*, has speculated on the indifference displayed by both FDR and

Churchill in the face of the Nazi Holocaust. Lookstein cites scholars who may dispute the use of the word "indifference" while pointing out that "Roosevelt's State Department actively opposed a large-scale rescue effort and that the British Foreign Office was actually fearful that a serious effort might be successful." Apparently, a successful rescue would have presented a touchy new problem: what to do with all those rescued Jews? Under Secretary of State for Special Problems Breckinridge Long went as far as charging the rescue advocates as subverting the war effort by acting as Berlin's agents.

"In the meantime," Lookstein adds, "Hitler's death camps were efficiently ensuring that fewer and fewer Jews would remain to be rescued."

"The rescue of European Jewry," writes Henry L. Feingold in *The Politics of Rescue*, "especially after the failure to act during the refugee phase (1939 to October 1941), was so severely circumscribed by Nazi determination that it would have required an inordinate passion to save lives and a huge reservoir of good will toward Jews to achieve it. Such passion to save Jewish lives did not exist in the potential receiving nations."

With a lack of public acknowledgement from the Roosevelt Administration, U.S. public opinion was not aroused. This, Feingold believes, convinced "men like Goebbels that the Allies approved or were at least indifferent to the fate of the Jews."

Goebbels's line of thinking was not too far from the truth. Even when eyewitness accounts from Auschwitz reached the U.S. Department of War and some in the Roosevelt Administration were pushing for the bombing of the death camp, or at least the railways leading to it, the word came down that air power could not be diverted from vital "industrial target system." It was claimed by American military planners, according to Feingold, that Auschwitz was "beyond the maximum range of medium bombardment, diver bombers and fighter bombers located in [the] United Kingdom, France or Italy."

After the war, it was common knowledge that Allied bombers passed within five miles of Auschwitz in August 1944.[17]

In March of 1943—a year in which the U.S. admitted only 23,775 immigrants into the country, the lowest figure in eighty years—Frida Kirchway, editor of *The Nation,* summed up the situation succinctly:

In this country, you and I, the President and the Congress and the State Department are accessories to the crime and share Hitler's guilt. If we behaved like humane and generous people instead of complacent cowardly ones, the two million lying today in the earth of Poland…would be alive and safe. We had it in our power to rescue this doomed people and yet we did not lift a hand to do it.[18]

When attempting to calculate the inherent goodness of the Allies in terms of their response to the Nazi Holocaust, one cannot ignore the post-war behavior of the Allied nations—in particular, the United States. For example, three months after V-E Day, radical journalist I.F. Stone reported that "many of the Jews and former slave laborers of the Nazis [were] living in the same concentration camps, fed a diet 'composed principally of bread and coffee,' still clothed in hideous concentration-camp garb or, even more ignominiously, in S.S. uniforms left behind by their oppressors." The former prisoners faced months without food in quarters "clearly unfit for winter use," yet ironically had to present grievances to German authorities because the Allied military government was not equipped to handle the situation. As Stone commented at the time, "The liberated are treated far worse than the defeated.[19]"

Even in 1946, well after the gut-wrenching images of gas chambers, mass graves, and emaciated death camp survivors had achieved worldwide notoriety, 72 percent of Americans still opposed allowing more Jewish refugees to live in the United

States.[20] For a dose of contemporary context, fast forward to 1993 and a *Newsweek* poll indicating that nearly 40 percent of adult Americans expressed "doubts as to whether a European Holocaust of the magnitude depicted in standard histories occurred during World War II.[21]"

DULLES'S LIST

Another prime opportunity for goodness to make a cameo appearance was the prosecution of Nazi war criminals. While specifics on the post-war relationships between the U.S. and its German POWs will be provided later, one aspect of this interaction remains relevant to any discussion of the weeks and months immediately following the liberation of Nazi death camps: Dulles's list.

Although Steven Spielberg's 1993 film, *Schindler's List*, offered a dramatic recreation of the forced labor camps, it did not fully depict the depth of the role played by German businessmen in perpetrating the slaughter. "The real Oskar Schindler's success in saving Jews depended upon one terrible reality," Christopher Simpson says. "[German] industry's cooperation with the genocide program was so complete, so pervasive, so taken for granted that Schindler could actually get away with a thousand Jews, and nobody would particularly notice.[22]"

Since corporations like BMW and Volkswagen profited mightily from the slave labor, one might expect the men who ran these and many, many other companies to face charges upon the war's end. That is where the list comes in. Not Schindler's list, but Dulles's list.

You recall Allen Dulles: Sullivan and Cromwell, meetings with Hitler, smoothing over Sosthenes Behn's treason, calling the Holocaust (in September 1942) "a wild rumor, inspired by Jewish fears.[23]"

During WWII, the younger Dulles brother headed the Office of Strategic Services (OSS), the precursor to the Central Intelligence Agency. After Hitler's suicide, says Simpson, Dulles "personally signed off on [a] list of German executives believed useful for restoring private enterprise in Central Europe. [He] sent messages to the U.S. authorities listing the names he wanted in high positions in postwar Germany. Dulles's lists are real, they're in the National Archives, and they're quite explicit.[24]"

Among the German bankers "rescued" by Allen Dulles was Karl Blessing, a business associate of Dulles's before the war. Blessing, a Nazi party member, was the youngest-ever Reichsbank director and a regular at Heinrich Himmler's meetings held to discuss industry's cooperation with the death camps. Blessing's company, Kontinental Oil, used Jews and Poles from the camps as slaves.

After the Nazi regime's surrender, Blessing's past was reinvented by Dulles. He was suddenly listed as a Nazi resister who deserved a position of influence in post-war Germany. This was not an isolated case. Telford Taylor, senior U.S. prosecutor at the Nuremberg Trials, admitted that prosecution of I.G. Farben executives was merely a symbolic gesture—a method of demonstrating the role of hundreds of companies in the perpetration of the Holocaust.[25]

It would be quite a leap of faith to suggest that the United States, having done next to nothing to stop the genocide, ever attempted to bring corporate murderers to justice after the war.

NEVER AGAIN?

If there is one group that might be able to rescue the "Good War" from the jaws of indifference and/or criminal collaboration, it must be that which suffered most. In the 1930s, as Hitler's actions against German Jews became known, some prominent American Jews suggested organizing a boycott of German goods. Irving Lehman (older brother of New York governor Herbert Lehman) spoke out against such a boycott. "I implore you," he pleaded, "don't let anger pass a resolution which will [bring harm to] Jews in Germany.²⁶" The record doesn't elaborate upon his definition of "harm."

The record does, however, offer some insight on those who were fighting for a Jewish homeland in the years leading up to WWII.

Further adding to the travesty of the term "Good War" is the knowledge that as WWII broke out, the main right-wing Jewish organization fighting the British mandate was a group called Irgun Zvai Leumi, inspired by the ideas of "moderate" Zionist Zev Jabotinsky (a moderate in that he only sought territory on "both sides of the River Jordan"). However, at the outset of the war, when Jabotinsky agreed to suspend military operations against Britain and even hinted at cooperating with them against the Nazis, Avraham Stern broke with Jabotinsky and formed the Stern Gang, "calling for a state that extended from the Nile to the Euphrates and proposing an alliance with Hitler to bring this about," according to journalist Christopher Hitchens. Stern's loyal deputy and eventual successor was none other than Yitzhak Yezernitsky, later known as Yitzhak Shamir.

In the fall of 1940, Stern met with one of Mussolini's agents in Jerusalem. By January, 1941, he put out feelers to the Nazis and dispatched an agent to meet with two of Hitler's emissaries in Beirut.

"Stern's proposal," explains Hitchens, "which was rashly put in writing, began by establishing his *ideological common ground with Nazism* (emphasis added), expressing sympathy with the Hitlerite goal of a Jew-free Europe and speaking of 'the goodwill of the German Reich government...toward Zionist activity inside Germany and towards the Zionist emigration plans.' "

Stern proposed the "establishment of the historical Jewish state on a national and totalitarian basis" and offered that he, Shamir, and the rest of the Stern Gang would "actively take part in the war on Germany's side."

As a result of this proposed alliance, Hitchens notes, members of Stern's group would react favorably—in public—to any news of Nazi victories. Even well into 1941, after Stern was killed in a shoot-out and as more and more became known of Nazi racial policies, Shamir took control of the Stern Gang—never renouncing its support for Hitler.[27]

Despite this, in 1986, Yitzhak Shamir became Prime Minister of Israel.

AN IMPROBABLE FICTION

Five decades after the horror, the corruption of the Holocaust was still playing a role in the shameful legacy of WWII. During one of the U.S. military's periodic spasms of saber-rattling towards Iraq, the November 15, 1998 *New York Post* gave ample space to the "heart-wrenching" reaction of a retired Israeli Air Force Colonel Zeev Leron.

"Again, gas masks? I cannot stand it!" Leron was responding to the reopening of gas-mask distribution centers in Israel. The colonel then went on to compare the current situation with his own time in a Nazi death camp.

"When I hear about gas masks in our Jewish state, everything comes back to me," said Leron. "The train stops, and I am again in Auschwitz...I stood facing Mengele."

What did this man learn from an unspeakable trauma? Did Col. Leron find meaning from his experiences? Judge for yourself.

"What kept me alive was the feeling of revenge: that I have to come out and kill these people," he explained to Uri Dan of the *Post*. "My main motivation to stay alive was to seek revenge from the Germans."

Leron's proposed solution to the U.S.-Iraq standoff is equally as enlightened: "Israel should eliminate [Saddam Hussein] physically. Israel should announce its decision publicly. The democratic world will understand.... Remembering the Holocaust, remembering that a third of our people have been eliminated in gas chambers, we have the right to declare this death sentence—and to not be threatened ever again with the trauma of gas masks in the

Jewish state."

Thus, genocide becomes the preeminent justification for assassination.

In April 1943, an editorial in the London *New Statesman and Nation* (later reprinted in the *Jewish Spectator*) contemplated the legacy of Allied indifference to the victims of the Nazi Holocaust, accurately predicting that "when historians relate this story of extermination, they will find it, from first to last, all but incredible."[28]

NOTES FOR CHAPTER THREE

1. The term "Roma" is used here instead of "Gypsy" because it is most often used by so-called Gypsies to describe themselves.

2. Haskell Lookstein; *Were We Our Brothers' Keepers? The Public Response of American Jews to the Holocaust, 1938-1944* (New York: Hartmore House, 1985) p. 29

3. The German Social Democratic Party (SPD) was one of three that made up the so-called Weimar Coalition in the 1920s (along with the German Democratic Party and the Catholic Center). Any resistance the SPD may have mustered against the rise of Nazism was sabotaged when Stalin pressured the Third Communist International in Moscow to incorrectly label the SPD "Social Fascists." Still, there was resistance from the German working class. Although Perry declares that "very few Germans realized that their country was passing through a long night of barbarism, and still fewer considered resistance," Michael Parenti reminds us that in both Germany and Italy "most workers and peasants made a firm distinction between fascism and communism, as did industrialists and bankers who supported fascism out of fear and hatred of communism, a judgment based largely on class realities." (p. 17)

4. Adams, p. 33

5. Ward Churchill. "Fascism, the FBI, & Native Americans," interviewed by David Barsamian, audiocassette, *Alternative Radio*, 1995

6. Adams, p. 83

7. Zinn, p. 406

8. D. Wright, p. 37

9. Agel & Glanze, p. 94

10. Adams, p. 120

11. Agel & Glanze, p. 94

12. Diane Yancey, *Life in a Japanese-American Internment Camp* (San Diego: Lucent Books, 1998) p. 10

13. Davis, p. 314

14. Mike Wright, p. 313

15. Arthur D. Morse; *While Six Million Died: A Chronicle of American Apathy* (Woodstock, NY: The Overlook Press, 1967) p. 27

16. Agel & Glanze, 86-7

17. Interviews with death camps survivors indicate that some railways were bombed but the Germans put the Jews to work in repairing them, thus making them targets.

18. Lookstein, p. 28. Other plans existed to save Jews by sending them to the French colony of Madagascar. FDR wanted to use Ethiopia, and one U.S. congressman suggested Alaska. All were eventually rejected.

19. I.F. Stone, *The War Years, 1939-1945* (Boston: Little Brown and Company, 1988) pp. 324-5. As noted by Noam Chomsky on p. 97 of *Chronicles of Dissent: Interviews with David Barsamian* (Monroe, ME: Common Courage Press, 1992), those death camp survivors who were able to reach the soon-to-be-established Jewish state in the late 1940s did not fare much better. The Zionist Organization sent many displaced persons (DP) to Jewish DP camps where they often died at almost the same rate they did under the Nazis.

20. Adams, p.147

21. Ward Churchill, "Assaults on Truth and Memory, Part I," *Z Magazine*, December 1996: pp. 31-37.

22. Spiegelman, pp. 13-18

23. John Weitz. *Hitler's Banker: Hjalmar Horace Greeley Schacht* (Boston: Little, Brown and Company 1997) p. 272

24. Spiegelman, pp. 13-18

25. Spiegelman, pp. 13-18 (for all references to German bankers in this section)

26. Herzstein, p. 108

27. While such right-wing Zionism was often opposed by Jewish socialists, Norman Finkelstein in *Image and Reality in the Israel-Palestine Conflict* (New York: Verso, 1995, 1997) says that, in the end, "Labor Zionism and the dissident right-wing Zionists organizations were in basic accord so far as the deployment of physical force against the Arabs were concerned." Labor Zionism, according to Finkelstein, "represented less an alternative than a supplement to political Zionism." (pp. 111, 9)

28. Lookstein, p. 29

CHAPTER FOUR

"Perhaps He is Human…"

OPPOSITE: AN AMERICAN CONCENTRATION CAMP FOR JAPANESE-AMERICANS.
Ordered from their homes in Los Angeles, this mix of one third Japanese aliens and two thirds U.S. Citizens await assignment to community homes in the Alien Reception Center at Manzanar, California.

*"Let these 'well-bred' gentry learn that we do with a clear conscience
the things they secretly do with a guilty one."*

—Adolf Hitler

Besides the rationale of ending the Holocaust, there is another explanation for WWII being a just war: the Japanese bombing of Pearl Harbor. To challenge this assumption, the "surprise attack" myth must be deconstructed. Also, an examination of the record as it pertains to U.S. attitudes and behavior towards the Japanese from the 1920s to the 1940s is required.

Western Civilization makes no specific mention of anti-Japanese bigotry while choosing to completely ignore the more than 100,000 Japanese-Americans imprisoned in internment camps. As for Pearl Harbor, Perry sticks to the party line and even manages to sneak in a little corporate boosterism while he's at it:

On December 7, 1941, the Japanese struck with carrier-based planes at Pearl Harbor in Hawaii. Taken by surprise, the Americans suffered total defeat.... After the attack on Pearl Harbor, Germany declared war on the United States. Now the immense American industrial capacity could be put to work against the Axis powers—Germany, Italy, and Japan.

Thus, today's student is yet again deprived of the context of anti-Japanese propaganda, e.g., a poll taken three days after the attack on Pearl Harbor that found 67 percent of Americans in favor of indiscriminate bombing of Japanese cities.[1] Nowhere in this text will the inquisitive of mind discover veteran socialist Norman Thomas's quote about the Pacific war being little more than an "organized race riot."

What were the events that led up to the bombing of Pearl Harbor? Why did U.S.-Japanese relations disintegrate in the 1930s? Did the United States take measures—both politically and economically—to provoke Japan? What was the general mood among Americans towards the Japanese before, during, and after WWII?

SURPRISE PARTY

The build-up to Pearl Harbor began two decades prior to the attack when, in 1922, the U.S., Britain, and Japan agreed that the Japanese navy would not be allowed more than 60 percent of the capital ship tonnage of the other two powers. As resentment grew within Japan over this decidedly inequitable agreement, that same year the United States Supreme Court declared Japanese immigrants ineligible for American citizenship. This decision was followed a year later by the Supreme Court upholding a California and Washington ruling denying Japanese the right to own property. A third judicial strike was dealt in 1924 with the Exclusion Act which virtually banned all Asian immigration. Finally, in 1930, when the London Naval Treaty denied Japan naval hegemony in its own waters, the groundwork for war (and "surprise attacks") had been laid.

Upon realizing that Japan textiles were outproducing Lancashire mills, the British Empire (including India, Australia, Burma, etc.) raised the tariff on Japanese exports by 25 percent.

Within a few years, the Dutch followed suit in Indonesia and the West Indies, with the U.S. (in Cuba and the Philippines) not far behind. This led to the Japanese (correctly) claiming encirclement by the "ABCD" (American, British, Chinese, and Dutch) powers.

Such moves, combined with Japan's expanding colonial designs, says Kenneth C. Davis, made "a clash between Japan and the United States and the other Western nations over control of the economy and resources of the Far East and Pacific...bound to happen."

WWII, in the Pacific theater, was essentially a war between colonial powers. It was not the Japanese invasion of China, the rape of Nanking, or the atrocities in Manchuria that resulted in the United States declaring war on the Empire of Japan. It was the attack of three of America's territories—the Philippines, Guam, and Hawaii (Pearl Harbor)—that provoked a military response.

The first military step on this road to war came to be known the *Panay* Incident. In 1937, the Japanese military forces occupying China ordered the sinking of all craft in China's longest river, the Yangtze (now called the Chang). One of the ships sunk was a U.S. gunboat, the *Panay*, which was on patrol with American oil tankers. The *Panay* was sunk on December 12. The Japanese apology came two days later. Interestingly, on the day in between—December 13—Japan attacked the city of Nanking and commenced to perpetrate of one of the war's most heinous crimes. The U.S., had it genuinely been interested in morality and justice, had a hostile act and massive human rights violations in consecutive days to use as a premise under which to demonstrate its noble intentions. The best that could be mustered by the arsenal of democracy was an increase in U.S. naval spending along with the first U.S.-British plans for naval cooperation, anticipating war with Japan over the rights to imperialist conquest.[2]

After the sinking of the *Panay*, a literal act of war, the concept of surprise should've been permanently abandoned—*four years* prior to Pearl Harbor. The exact date, time, and place may not have been known but, short of a major mobilization by the international working class, the U.S. was clearly on a collision course with Japan once the burgeoning Asian empire began interfering with American colonies throughout Southeast Asia.

The Great Depression hit Japan too, and like all military powers, they chose to rely on colonialism as a form of relief. Claiming a sort of "Monroe Doctrine" of their own, when France fell to Germany, the Japanese moved quickly to take military control of French colonies in Indochina (the main source for most U.S. tin and rubber).

On July 21, 1941, Japan signed a preliminary agreement with the Nazi-sympathizing Vichy government of Marshal Henri Pétain, leading to Japanese occupation of airfields and naval bases in Indochina. Almost immediately, the U.S., Britain, and the Netherlands instituted a total embargo on oil and scrap metal to Japan—tantamount to a declaration of war. This was followed soon after by the United States and Great Britain freezing all Japanese assets in their respective countries. Radhabinod Pal, one of the judges in the post-war Tokyo War Crimes Tribunal, later argued that the U.S. had clearly provoked the war with Japan, calling the embargoes a "clear and potent threat to Japan's very existence."[3]

Further exacerbating matters, as Michael C.C. Adams reports, in November 1941, the U.S. sent $100 million to Chinese nationalists to buy arms. This was security against both Japanese encroachment on American colonies and the growing communist revolution within China itself.

The attack on Pearl Harbor earned Japan a reputation as "treacherous," a tag that justified many war crimes and lasted well past the bombing of Hiroshima and Nagasaki. However, before accepting such a racist stereotype someone should have at least provided some evidence of treachery.

The above passages depict the disposition of the U.S.-Japan relationship in the years leading up to Pearl Harbor—a temper illustrated by one theory surrounding the disappearance of aviator Amelia Earhart. Almost from the moment her plane vanished in

1937, there were those who believed that Earhart was killed or taken prisoner by belligerent Japanese. Historian William Manchester has hypothesized that Earhart, while flying over the Marianas in the Pacific, caught sight of the illegal Japanese fortifications under construction on the string of islands and was "almost certainly forced down and murdered," a theory that has never been proven to be false.[4]

How then, under conditions hostile enough to spawn such immediate speculation, could any military attack be genuinely categorized as a surprise and thus an act of treachery? If the U.S. wasn't expecting trouble, why did Army Chief of Staff George C. Marshall request plans *before* Pearl Harbor for "general incendiary attacks to burn up the wood and paper structures of the densely populated Japanese cities"?[5]

As historian Thomas A. Bailey has written: "Franklin Roosevelt repeatedly deceived the American people during the period before Pearl Harbor…. He was like the physician who must tell the patient lies for the patient's own good."[6]

The diplomatic record reveals some of what Dr. Roosevelt neglected to tell his easily-deluded patients in that now-mythical "Date of Infamy" speech[7]:

- Dec. 14, 1940: Joseph Grew, U.S. Ambassador to Japan, sends a letter to FDR, announcing that, "It seems to me increasingly clear that we are bound to have a showdown [with Japan] some day."

- Dec. 30, 1940: Pearl Harbor is considered so likely a target of Japanese attack that Rear Admiral Claude C. Bloch, commander of the Fourteenth Naval District, authors a memorandum entitled, "Situation Concerning the Security of the Fleet and the Present Ability of the Local Defense Forces to Meet Surprise Attacks."

- Jan. 27, 1941: Grew (in Tokyo) sends a dispatch to the State Department: "My Peruvian Colleague told a member of my staff that the Japanese military forces planned, in the event of trouble with the United States, to attempt a surprise mass attack on Pearl Harbor using all of their military facilities."

• Feb. 5, 1941: Bloch's December 30, 1940 memorandum leads to much discussion and eventually a letter from Rear Admiral Richmond Kelly Turner to Secretary of War Henry Stimson in which Turner warns, "The security of the U.S. Pacific Fleet while in Pearl Harbor, and of the Pearl Harbor Naval Base itself, has been under renewed study by the Navy Department and forces afloat for the past several weeks.... If war eventuates with Japan, it is believed easily possible that hostilities would be initiated by a surprise attack upon the Fleet or the Naval Base at Pearl Harbor.... In my opinion, the inherent possibilities of a major disaster to the fleet or naval base warrant taking every step, as rapidly as can be done, that will increase the joint readiness of the Army and Navy to withstand a raid of the character mentioned above."

• Feb. 18, 1941: Commander in Chief, Admiral Husband E. Kimmel says, "I feel that a surprise attack on Pearl Harbor is a possibility."

• Sept. 11, 1941: Kimmel says, "A strong Pacific Fleet is unquestionably a deterrent to Japan—a weaker one may be an invitation."

• Nov. 25, 1941: Secretary of War Henry L. Stimson writes in his diary that, "The President...brought up entirely the relations with the Japanese. He brought up the event that we're likely to be attacked [as soon as] next Monday for the Japanese are notorious for making an attack without warning."

• Nov. 27, 1941: U.S. Army Chief of Staff George C.

Marshall issues a memorandum cautioning that "Japanese future action unpredictable but hostile action possible at any moment. If hostilities cannot…be avoided, the United States desires that Japan commit the first overt action."

• Nov 29, 1941: Secretary of State Cordell Hull, responding to a speech by Japanese General Hideki Tojo one week before the attack, phones FDR at Warm Springs, GA to warn of "the imminent danger of a Japanese attack," and urge him to return to Washington sooner than planned.

Regardless of this record, there were still racists within the U.S. military and government who never imagined that Japan could orchestrate such a successful offensive. Few Westerners took the Japanese seriously, with journalists regularly referring to them as "apes in khaki" during the early months of their conquest of Southeast Asia. The simian metaphor was maintained thereafter.[8] This racist attitude continued on as the two sides approached war—with unexpected consequences

"Most American military minds expected a Japanese attack to come in the Philippines, America's major base in the Pacific," writes Davis. "Many Americans, including Roosevelt, dismissed the Japanese as combat pilots because they were all presumed to be 'near-sighted'…. There was also a sense that any attack on Pearl Harbor would be easily repulsed." Such an attitude appears even more ludicrous in light of the pre-Pearl Harbor record of the Japanese fighter pilots flying the world's most advanced fighter plane, the Mitsubishi Zero.[9]

"The first actual combat test of the Zero occurred in September 1940," reports historian John W. Dower, "when thirteen of the planes downed twenty-seven Chinese aircraft in ten minutes." By August 31, 1941, thirty Japanese Zeros "accounted for 266 confirmed kills in China." Still, the American military planners were somehow shocked by the skill displayed by the Japanese at Pearl Harbor.

Shortly after the attack, with the image of a uniquely treacherous enemy spread throughout America, Admiral William Halsey, soon to become commander of the South Pacific Force, vowed that by the end of the war, "Japanese would be spoken only in hell." His favorite slogan "Kill Japs, kill Japs, kill more Japs" echoed the sentiments of Admiral William D. Leahy, chair of the Joint Chiefs of Staff, who wrote that "in fighting with Japanese savages, all previously accepted rules of warfare must be abandoned."[10]

VERMIN AND SOUVENIRS

Because Japan chose to invade several colonial outposts of the West, the war in the Pacific laid bare the inherent racism of the colonial structure. In the United States and Britain, the Japanese were more hated than the Germans. The race card was played to the hilt through a variety of Allied propaganda methods. Spurred on by a growing Chinese lobby and vocal American trade protectionists wary of inexpensive Japanese goods, the campaign would eventually help cajole the American public into a pro-war, anti-Japan position. By 1938, as Adams writes, polls showed more Americans favored military aid to China than to Britain or France. Even more so than the Third Reich, Japan was the U.S. villain of choice.

"Periodicals that regularly featured accounts of Japanese atrocities," says Dower, "gave negligible coverage to the genocide of the Jews, and the Holocaust was not even mentioned in the *Why We Fight* [film] series Frank Capra directed for the U.S. Army."

The Japanese soldiers (and, for that matter, all Japanese) were commonly referred to and depicted as subhuman—insects, monkeys, apes, rodents, or simply barbarians that must be wiped out or exterminated. The *American Legion Magazine*'s cartoon of monkeys in a zoo who had posted a sign reading, "Any similarity between us and the Japs is purely coincidental" was typical.[11] A U.S. Army poll in 1943 found that roughly half of all GIs believed it would be necessary to kill every Japanese on earth before peace could be achieved. Their superiors in Washington appeared to agree. By December 1943, as Adams notes, there were more troops and equipment in the Pacific than in Europe and it has been estimated that 1,589 artillery rounds were fired to kill each Japanese soldier.

As a December 1945 *Fortune* poll revealed, American feelings for the Japanese did not soften after the war. Nearly twenty-three percent of those questioned wished the U.S. could have dropped "many more [atomic bombs] before the Japanese had a chance to surrender."[12]

This virulent brand of genocidal hatred was the end result of a massive public relations effort to demonize the enemy in the Pacific and thereby justify *anything* in the name of victory. A fine example could be found in the *New York Times* when the newspaper of record ran an ad that showed a flame-thrower being used to kill Japanese, bearing the headline: "Clearing Out a Rats' Nest."[13]

With generals like the Australian Sir Thomas Blamey informing his troops that, "Beneath the thin veneer of a few generations of civilization, [the Japanese] is a subhuman beast," the feeding frenzy of ignorance and race antagonism culminated in the Allied forces acting our their predetermined role in a self-fulfilling prophecy. If a subhuman will fight to the death like an animal, those fighting on the side of good were simply left with no alternative but to slaughter them unmercifully. Since Japanese soldiers were under pressure not to surrender and were often killed when they did, this became a self-fulfilling prophecy.

General Blamey later told the *New York Times* that "fighting Japs is not like fighting normal human beings. The Jap is a little barbarian…. We are not dealing with humans as we know them. We are dealing with something primitive. Our troops have the right view of the Japs. They regard them as vermin."

This dissertation was quoted by the *Times* on the front page.[14]

Eugene B. Sledge, author of *With the Old Breed at Peleliu and Okinawa*, and now a biologist, wrote of his comrades "harvesting gold teeth" from the enemy dead. In Okinawa, Sledge witnessed "the most repulsive thing I ever saw an American do in the war"—

when a Marine officer stood over a Japanese corpse and urinated into its mouth.

There was no shortage of horror stories about Japanese atrocities to fuel such animosity and a large part of them *were* true. Of the 235,473 U.S. and U.K. prisoners reported captured by Germany and Italy combined, only 4 percent (9,348) died while an astonishing 27 percent of Japan's Anglo-American POWs (35,756 of 132,134) did not survive.[15] Indeed, with the rape of Nanking, the Bataan Death March, and incidents such as when Marines on Guadalcanal were ambushed by Japanese soldiers pretending to surrender, the litany of Japanese war crimes did not need much embellishment to stir up Allied fury. The ensuing behavior of the men fighting the Japanese in the Pacific (and those rooting for them back home) was merely the anticipated outcome of a deadly campaign of manipulation and propaganda against an enemy which often played right into those fears. The results, however predictable, are no less appalling.

"In April 1943," Dower reports, "the *Baltimore Sun* ran a story about a local mother who had petitioned authorities to permit her son to mail her an ear he had cut off a Japanese soldier in the South Pacific. She wished to nail it to her front door for all to see."

In a 1943 issue of *Leatherneck*, the Marine monthly, a photo of Japanese corpses was run above the caption: "GOOD JAPS are dead Japs."[16] The March 15, 1943 issue of *Time* followed suit by reporting without criticism about a "low-flying fighter turning lifeboats towed by motor barges and packed with Jap survivors, into bloody sieves."

Where is such behavior spawned? One breeding ground is boot camp. Consider this U.S. Marine Corps boot camp chant:

Rape the town and kill the people, that's the thing we love to do! Rape the town and kill the people, that's the only thing to do! Watch the kiddies scream and shout, rape the town and kill the people, that's the thing we love to do![17]

Perhaps Edgar L. Jones, a former war correspondent in the Pacific, put it best when he asked in the February 1946 *Atlantic Monthly,* "What kind of war do civilians suppose we fought anyway? We shot prisoners in cold blood, wiped out hospitals, strafed lifeboats, killed or mistreated enemy civilians, finished off the enemy wounded, tossed the dying into a hole with the dead, and in the Pacific boiled flesh off enemy skulls to make table ornaments for sweethearts, or carved their bones into letter openers."[18]

The "official" word was equally as repugnant:

Elliot Roosevelt, the president's son and confidant, told Henry Wallace in 1945 that America should bomb Japan "until we have destroyed about half the Japanese civilian population." Paul V. McNutt, chairman of the War Manpower Commission, went a little further when he advocated to a public audience in April 1945 the "extermination of the Japanese in toto."[19] Secretary of War Henry Stimson concurred, stating that "to get on with Japan, one had to treat her rough, unlike other countries."[20] That these sentiments were often translated into action is borne out in the reality that the U.S. bombers killed four to five times as many civilians in the last five months of the Pacific war than in three years of Allied bombing in Europe combined. And then there was the man who'd eventually give the order to drop atomic bombs on Japanese civilians.

"We have used [the bomb] against those who have abandoned all pretense of obeying international laws of warfare," Harry Truman later explained, thus justifying his decision to nuke a people that he termed "savages, ruthless, merciless, and fanatic."[21]

Such rhetoric and the comportment it spawned was encouraged, according to Dower, by three basic rationalizations. First, the "suicide psychology" involved the myth that since the fanatical Japanese would rather die than surrender, they "invited destruction." The second rationalization had its roots in the First World War and the treaty that ended it. "Anything less than a thoroughgoing defeat" would be "incomplete" and invite the Japanese to use peace as a chance to prepare for war—like the Germans did between the two world wars. Finally, the "psychological purge" evoked the concept of the Japanese requiring castigation in the form of "great destruction and suffering." As Alger Hiss explained at the time, "[Japan's] entire national psychology [must] be radically modified."

The inherently racist premises behind these three rationalizations eerily evoke the justifications often proffered for the extermination of Native Americans or the enslavement of Africans. Two decades after the end of the "Good War," the U.S. was still getting mileage from what became known as the "mere gook rule."

"During the Vietnam War," writes Edward S. Herman, "it was reported that cynical U.S. lawyers working in that country had coined the phrase 'mere gook rule' to describe the very lenient treatment given to U.S. military personnel who killed Vietnamese civilians." This policy held sway right on through various American interventions in Latin America, the "humanitarian" effort in Somalia, and, of course, the Gulf War and Kosovo. Herman sums up the philosophy as follows: "If our opponents do not submit and we are obliged to blow them up, clearly it is their responsibility."[22]

Of course, for the men doing the actual fighting, it essentially comes down to the most basic of racist tenets. In order to inflict inhumane punishment, it is necessary to convince oneself that the enemy is not fully human. Once that belief is established, slavery, genocide, and the boiling of flesh off of Japanese skulls to be saved as souvenirs have all the justification they will ever need.

THE SPIRIT OF ST. CHARLES

Rationality in the Pacific was so rare during World War II that, ironically, it required as a mouthpiece none other than prominent racist Colonel Charles A. Lindbergh, Jr. Repelled by what he saw and heard of U.S. treatment of the Japanese in the Pacific theater, the aviator spoke out. His sentiments are summed up in the following journal entry:

> It was freely admitted that some of our soldiers tortured Jap prisoners and were as cruel and barbaric at times as the Japs themselves. Our men think nothing of shooting a Japanese prisoner or a soldier attempting to surrender. They treat the Jap with less respect than they would give to an animal, and these acts are condoned by almost everyone. We claim to be fighting for civilization, but the more I see of this war in the Pacific the less right I think we have to claim to be civilized.[23]

"When Lindbergh finally left the Pacific islands and cleared customs in Hawaii," says Dower, "he was asked if he had any [Japanese] bones in his baggage. It was, he was told, a routine question."[24]

AMERICAN CONCENTRATION CAMPS

Contrary to Professor Perry's college text, no discussion of WWII in general or the war in the Pacific in particular, could possibly be complete with examining the U.S. internment of Japanese-Americans.

In February 1942, Franklin Delano Roosevelt signed Executive Order 9066 giving the army the unrestricted power to arrest—without warrants or indictments or hearings—every Japanese-American on a 150-mile strip along the West Coast (roughly 110,000 men, women, and children) and transport them to internment camps in Colorado, Utah, Arkansas, and other interior states to be kept under prison conditions. This order was upheld by the Supreme Court and the Japanese-Americans remained in custody for over three years.

Thanks to an unending wave of anti-Japan propaganda, there

was little public debate over this immoral crime. In fact, in 1942, a *Los Angeles Times* writer defended the forced relocations by explaining to his readers that "a viper is nonetheless a viper wherever the egg is hatched—so a Japanese-American, born of Japanese parents, grows up to be a Japanese, not an American."[25] In nearby countries, sentiments ran along these same lines, as Daniel S. Davis reports in *Behind Barbed Wire*:

> Canada enacted similar removal and internment programs.... Many Latin American countries were shaken by anti-Japanese riots. Some shipped their Japanese people to the United States at the urging of Washington. They were held in the camps our government set up.... Ironically, after the war ended, the U.S. government tried to deport these Latin American Japanese on the grounds that they had entered the country without passports or official visas.

Life in the internment camps entailed cramped living spaces with communal meals and bathrooms. The one-room apartments measured twenty by twenty feet and none had running water. The internees were allowed to take along "essential personal effects" from home but were prohibited from bringing razors, scissors, or radios. Outside the shared wards were barbed wire, guard towers with machine guns, and searchlights. The atmosphere was often charged with a hostile discomfort.

Anger and disillusionment grew and these emotions led to tension and sometimes violence. On December 5, 1942, a scuffle between internees led to the U.S. military police firing shots into the crowd—killing one Japanese-American man, Jimmy Ito.[26]

There were those who defied relocation. Fred Korematsu remained in San Francisco with his Caucasian girlfriend until he was arrested and jailed. It was then that he met with an ACLU lawyer and decided to challenge the constitutionality of the internment camps. He lost when the Supreme Court upheld the decision in December 1944. Justice Murphy, expressing a minority opinion, dissented, noting that the camps were "an obvious racial discrimination, the order deprives all those within its scope of equal protection of the laws guaranteed by the Fifth Amendment."[27]

While 110,000 Japanese-Americans suffered in prison camps, the U.S. media whipped up a post-Pearl Harbor frenzy of fear on the West Coast. If one was to believe the news reports of the day, it would seem that it was always just a matter of hours until Japanese Zeros would be spotted over Hollywood—or anywhere on the Left Coast. In January 1942, Edward R. Murrow stirred up fifth column worries by telling an audience in Seattle that if their city was ever bombed, they would "be able to look up and see some University of Washington sweaters on the boys doing the bombing."[28]

Despite widespread concerns of Japanese infiltration, an FBI report admitted:

> We have not found a single machine gun, nor have we found any gun in any circumstances indicating that it was to be used in a manner helpful to our enemies. We have not found a single camera which we have reason to believe was for use in espionage.[29]

Although there was never a proven case of any type of sabotage by Japanese-Americans on the West Coast, this did little to ease the minds of men like California attorney general Earl Warren (later the chief justice of the U.S. Supreme Court). "I believe that we are just being lulled into a false sense of security," Warren declared, "and that the only reason we haven't had disaster in California is because it has been timed for a different date."[30]

The dislocated Japanese-Americans incurred an estimated loss of $400 million in forced property sales during the internment years, and therein may lie a more Machiavellian motivation than sheer race hatred.

"A large engine for the Japanese-American incarcerations was agri-business," says Michio Kaku, a noted nuclear physicist and political activist whose parents were interned from 1942 to 1946.

"Agri-businesses in California coveted much of the land owned by Japanese-Americans."[31]

A formal apology came to the 60,000 survivors of internment camps in 1990. The U.S. government paid them each $20,000.[32]

While Yale Law Professor Eugene V. Rostow later called the internment camps "our worst wartime mistake," Howard Zinn pointedly asks: "Was it a 'mistake'—or was it an action to be expected from a nation with a long history of racism and which was fighting a war, not to end racism, but to retain the fundamentals of the American system?"

Not all Japanese spent WWII in American concentration camps. Over 12,000 Japanese-Americans—or *Nisei*—actually fought in the U.S. Army (that is, after Eleanor Roosevelt had their initial classification of "enemy alien" reversed in June 1942). However, while one-third of these troops amazingly volunteered directly from the internment camps, the racism didn't end just because they now wore a GI uniform. Journalist Tom Dunkel has reported that General Dwight D. Eisenhower "declined to have any Nisei under his command." Lt. Gen. John J. DeWitt, the army's West Coast military commander at the time, bluntly noted why, "A Jap's a Jap."

Things didn't exactly improve after the war for the Nisei vets. It wasn't until 1997 that a Japanese-American veteran of WWII was awarded a Medal of Honor.

"I know it was prejudice. Absolutely," admits Gene Castagnetti, the director of the National Memorial Cemetery of the Pacific in Honolulu. "From 1941 to 1945, we demonized everything Japanese. How were we going to award this nation's top honor for bravery to Americans of Japanese ancestry?"

"Looking back," Stanley Akita, a Japanese-American soldier with the 100th Infantry Battalion told Dunkel, "a lot of the boys feel we were cannon fodder."[33]

Immediately after Japan's defeat, the transformation from either cannon fodder or rodents to valuable anti-communist allies commenced. Again, the Cold War actually started amidst the hot war in 1917, and this was remarkably consistent with U.S. actions in the Soviet Union after WWII.

"The ink on the Japanese surrender treaty was hardly dry when the United States began to use the Japanese soldiers still in China alongside American troops in a joint effort against the Chinese communists," writes William Blum. Even the anti-Mao armies of Chiang Kai-shek contained Japanese units. President Truman saw it like this:

> It was perfectly clear to us that if we told the Japanese to lay down their arms immediately and march to the seaboard, [China] would be taken over by the Communists.[34]

In the Philippines, with the U.S. seeking to squash the anti-imperialist resistance army—the Huks—it was again prudent to exorcise yesterday's demon. "The Japanese were allowed to assault Huk forces unmolested," says Blum. Similar tactics were deployed in Korea and Vietnam; recent history has recorded the result of those endeavors.

All in all, the racist justifications for imperialist warfare have essentially remained the same, it's only the targets that change according to need.

FOR GOOD MEASURE

Japan's transition from a primitive nation of treacherous apes to a reliable anti-communist bulwark obviously carried an exorbitantly high price. Even as the second atomic bomb was being dropped on Nagasaki on August 9, 1945, and Japanese surrender became a matter of sheer formality, the activities of the "Good War" continued undiminished. A total of sixteen U.S. airmen were summarily executed in Japan while the U.S. was busy supplying what General Henry "Hap" Arnold called "as big a finale as possible."

The *New York Daily News* of August 15, 1945 reported unambiguously on the timing of such raids: "Nearly 400 B-29 Superfortresses, attacking 12 hours after Japan said its capitulation message was Washington-bound, blasted targets in the Jap homeland."

Living out his dream to hit Tokyo with a 1,000-plane raid, Arnold sent 1,104 aircraft out on the night of August 14. They bombed Tokyo without a single loss. Leonard Dietz was one of the pilots who flew in Hap Arnold's finale.

"I remember looking down—we were at 23,000 feet—and we could see nothing of the city of Tokyo because it was leveled," Dietz recalled. "It was like a giant hand had come out of the sky and mashed everything to the ground. It looked like it was hit by an atomic bomb."[35] Before all of Arnold's planes had returned to their bases, Truman was announcing Japan's unconditional surrender.

How does a nation supposedly fighting on the side of good during a supposedly good war exonerate such premeditated carnage? As *Time* magazine explained, while reporting on the battle of Iwo Jima (a battle in which the popular magazine referred to the U.S. Marines as "rodent exterminators"), it's all just a matter of perspective: "The ordinary unreasoning Jap is ignorant. Perhaps he is human. Nothing…indicates it."[36]

NOTES FOR CHAPTER FOUR

1. Stephen Shalom, "V-J Day: Remembering the Pacific War," *Z Magazine* July/August 1995, p. 76
2. Agel & Glanze, p. 92
3. Zinn, p. 402
4. K. Davis, p. 285. While speculation on this theory still persists, Japanese complicity in Earhart's disappearance has never been proven. Regardless, the existence of such conjecture in 1937 serves as a valid measure of America's suspicious and hostile attitude towards Japan in the years prior to the attack on Pearl Harbor.
5. Shalom, p. 76
6. Zinn, p. 402
7. Gordon William Prange. *At Dawn We Slept: The Untold Story of Pearl Harbor* (New York: Viking, 1991). The following Pearl Harbor timetable can be attributed to Prange's diligent research.
8. John W. Dower. *War Without Mercy: Race & Power in the Pacific War* (New York, Pantheon Books, 1986) p. 84
9. Davis, p. 293
10. Halsey quote, Dower, p. 36. Leahy quote, Shalom, p. 75. Halsey's motto appeared on the cover of the July 23, 1945 issue of *Time* in which the admiral proclaimed: "I hate Japs. I'm telling you men that if I met a pregnant Japanese woman, I'd kick her in the belly."
11. Dower, pp. 53, 87
12. Dower, p. 54. A poll taken during the war asked Americans which nation could the U.S. "get along better with after the war." 92 percent chose Germany while only 8 percent said Japan.
13. Adams, p. 74
14. Dower, p. 53
15. Dower, p. 48
16. Dower, p. 79
17. Daniel William Hallock. *Hell, Healing and Resistance: Veterans Speak* (Farmington, PA: The Plough Publishing House, 1998) p. 33
18. Shalom, p. 76
19. Dower, p. 55
20. Scott, audiocassette
21. Ronald Takaki. *Hiroshima: Why America Dropped the Atomic Bomb* (Boston: Little, Brown and Company, 1995) p. 100
22. Edward S. Herman. *Beyond Hypocrisy: Decoding*

the News in the Age of Propaganda (Boston: South End Press, 1992), pp. 54-5, 153

23. Stromberg, audiocassette

24. Dower, p. 71

25. Yancey, p. 27.

26. Yancey, p. 78.

27. Yancey, p. 74.

28. Yancey, p. 27.

29. Yancey, pp. 27-8.

30. M. Wright , p. 166.

31. Michio Kaku, "Legacy of Nuclear Weapons," interviewed by David Barsamian, audiocassette, *Alternative Radio*, 1995. Kaku estimates that the land appropriated from Japanese-Americans is today worth "hundreds of billions of dollars."

32. M. Wright, p. 171

33. Tom Dunkel. "Small Soldiers," *George*, August 1998, pp. 99-101, 108-9

34. Blum, p. 21

35. Dower, p. 301

36. Wittner, p. 105

CHAPTER FIVE

"A New Kind of Weather..."

OPPOSITE: Two marines of the Sixth Marine Division flush Japanese soldiers out of an underground tunnel in Southern Okinawa. One marine wields a flame-thrower, the other a rifle to fire at any soldiers who get through the flames.

"Anonymous mass destruction was the dominant characteristic."

—Historian Michael C.C. Adams

he March 19, 1990 issue of *Newsweek*, in the course of discussing America's supposedly reduced commitment to NATO, offered the following commentary: "As America pulls back from the European theater it entered on D-Day, it will mean loosening ties with the last battlefield where U.S. military might was a symbol of unalloyed good, free of the moral and political ambiguities of Vietnam, Grenada, Lebanon, or Panama."

The oblivious editors of *Newsweek* were topped, however, by FDR's rhetoric immediately after the German blitzkreig of Poland in September 1939.

The ruthless bombing from the air of civilians in unfortified centers of population during the course of the hostilities which have raged in various quarters of the earth during the past few years, which has resulted in the maiming and the death of thousands of defenseless men, women, and children, has sickened the hearts of every civilized man and woman, and has profoundly shocked the conscience of humanity.[1]

Or perhaps, it was the reaction of U.S. Secretary of State

Cordell Hull upon hearing of the fascist bombing of civilians in Barcelona that set the popular newsweekly swooning. "No theory of war can justify such conduct," Hull crowed nobly.[2]

Indeed, these are appropriate sentiments for those allegedly representing "unalloyed good"; for those supposedly free from moral and political ambiguity.

Often cited as the unassailable confirmation that the Allies were truly warriors in a good war is the comparison with the unspeakable horrors of the Axis. But what happens when the *good guys* are proven to have behaved—consistently and purposefully—in a manner often indistinguishable from the forces of evil? How does that fit into the "Good War" mythology?

While some criminal acts, e.g. shooting Japanese prisoners, have already been discussed in earlier chapters, the following discussions will shed further light on the inevitable elements of war (good or otherwise).

READY...AIM...

"In mid-1941 the British abandoned the illusion that they could hit military-industrial targets with surgical strikes," writes historian Michael C.C. Adams. This was the decision of one Marshal Arthur Harris, the director of England's Bomber Command. Harris, nicknamed "Bomber," mastered the ins and outs of committing war crimes from his insidious instructor, Winston Churchill.

The year was 1919, according to journalist Alexander Cockburn, "when the Royal Air Force asked Churchill for permission to use chemical weapons 'against recalcitrant Arabs as an experiment.'" Churchill, secretary of state at the war office at the time, promptly consented.[3]

"I am strongly in favor of using poisoned gas against uncivilized tribes," he explained, a policy he espoused yet again in July 1944 when he asked his chiefs of staff to consider using poison gas on the Germans "or any other method of warfare we have hitherto refrained from using." Unlike in 1919, his proposal was denied. [4]

Anyone who had consulted Churchill's record would not have been surprised by his predisposition towards attacking those he deemed inferior. In 1910, in the capacity of Home Secretary, he "secretly proposed the sterilization of 100,000 'mental degenerates' and the dispatch of tens of thousands of others to state-run labor camps," reports Cockburn. These actions were to take place in the name of saving the British race from inevitable decline as its inferior members bred.

One can imagine *der Führer*'s proud smile.

"They [the Arabs and Kurds] now know what real bombing means, in casualties and damage," declared the aforementioned Bomber Harris, air force officer at the time of Sir Winston's 1919 decision to poison the uncivilized tribes in the Middle East.[5]

Harris and Churchill teamed up again some twenty-five years later to execute a relentless terror bombing campaign during WWII for which Harris offered no apologies and demonstrated no qualms. His attitude was best displayed when, during the later stages of the war, Harris was stopped by a motorcycle policeman while speeding in his car.

"You might have killed someone, sir," came the reprimand, to which Bomber Harris replied, "Young man, I kill thousands of people every night."[6]

One can imagine Churchill's proud smile.

As for the Americans in the European theater, under direct orders from President Roosevelt, U.S. bombers initially stuck to a slightly more humane policy of daylight precision bombing. Unlike their British counterparts, Americans did not have images of the Luftwaffe over London to motivate them towards unabashed mass murder; it took them a little longer to reach the point of mass murder as policy.

However, the risks of daylight bombing runs did not pay off in accuracy—only 50 percent of U.S. bombs fell within a quarter of a mile of the target. America soon joined their English allies in the execution of nighttime area bombing campaigns of civilian targets in Germany.

The saturation bombardment of Bomber Harris and his American counterparts resulted in at least 635,000 dead German civilians.[7]

Day or night, the myth of precision was easily debunked by the great number of shells falling where they were not aimed. A July 24 and 25, 1944 bombing operation called COBRA called for 1,800 U.S. bombers to hit German defenders near Saint-Lô. The planes arrived one day early and bombed so inaccurately that twenty-five Americans were killed and 131 wounded—causing some U.S. units to open fire on their own aircraft. The next day, with the American soldiers withdrawn thousands of yards to avoid a repeat performance, the bombers still missed their mark and ended up killing 111 GIs and wounding nearly 500 more.[8]

"In order to invade the Continent," says historian Paul Fussell, "the Allies killed 12,000 innocent French and Belgian civilians who happened to live in the wrong part of town, that is, too near the railway tracks."

Even when the target was hit, the results could be horrific. In October 1944, the U.S. submarine *Snook* torpedoed and sunk the Japanese merchant vessel *Arisan Maru*. However, the *Arisan Maru* was carrying thousands of American prisoners being taken from the Philippines to Japan for safety. They all drowned.[9]

In 1945, Britain and America added even more fuel to the fire.

DEATH FROM ABOVE (PART ONE)

On February 13–14, 1945, Allied bombers laid siege to the German town of Dresden—once known as "Florence on the Elbe." With the Russians advancing rapidly towards Berlin, tens of thousands of German civilians fled into Dresden, believing it to be safe from attack. As a result, the city's population swelled from its usual 600,000 to at least one million.[10]

Following up a smaller raid on Hamburg in July 1943 that killed at least 48,000 civilians, Winston Churchill enlisted the aid of British scientists to cook up "a new kind of weather." The goal was not only maximum destruction and loss of life, but also to show their communist allies what a capitalist war machine could do, in case Stalin had any crazy ideas.

An internal Royal Air Force memo described the anti-communist plans as such:

> Dresden, the seventh largest city in Germany and not much smaller than Manchester, is also [by] far the largest unbombed built-up area the enemy has got. In the midst of winter, with refugees pouring westwards and troops to be rested, roofs are at a premium, not only to give shelter…but to house the administrative services displaced from other areas…. The intentions of the attack are to hit the enemy where he will feel it most…and to show the Russians when they arrive what Bomber Command can do.[11]

There was never any doubt on the part of the Allies exactly who they would be bombing at Dresden. Brian S. Blades, a flight engineer in a Lancaster of 460 (Australian) Squadron, wrote that during briefings, he heard phrases like "Virgin target," and "Intelligence reports thousands of refugees streaming into the city from other bombed areas."[12]

Beside the stream of refugees, Dresden was also known for its china and its Baroque and Rococo architecture. Its galleries housed works by Vermeer, Rembrandt, Rubens, and Botticelli. In addition, Grosser Garten contained the extremely popular Dresden Zoo, run by famous animal trainer, Otto Sailer-Jackson.

On the evening of February 13, none of this would matter.

Using the Dresden soccer stadium as a reference point, over 2000 British Lancasters and American Flying Fortresses dropped loads of gasoline bombs every 50 square yards out from this marker. The enormous flame that resulted was eight square miles wide, shooting smoke three miles high. For the next eighteen hours, regular bombs were dropped on top of this strange brew. Twenty-five minutes after the bombing, winds reaching 150 miles-per-hour sucked everything into the heart of the storm. Because the air became superheated and rushed upward, the fire lost most of its oxygen, creating tornadoes of flame that can suck the air right out of human lungs.

Seventy percent of the Dresden dead either suffocated or died from poison gases that turned their bodies green and red. The intense heat melted some bodies into the pavement like bubblegum, or shrunk them into three-foot long charred carcasses. Clean-up crews wore rubber boots to wade through the "human soup" found in nearby caves. In other cases, the superheated air propelled victims skyward only to come down in tiny pieces as far as fifteen miles outside Dresden.

As stated earlier, the Allied fire-bombing is believed to have killed more than 100,000 people, mostly civilians. But the exact number may never be known due to the high number of refugees in the area.

At the Dresden Zoo, Sailer-Jackson was forced to consider the standing Nazi order that if human life was endangered, all carnivores must be shot. But before he could take the lives of his beloved big cats, a new wave of bombers set the zoo ablaze. The animal trainer recalled the scene for historian Alexander McKee:

> The elephants gave spine-chilling screams. Their house was still standing but an explosive bomb of terrific force had landed behind it, lifted the dome of the house, turned it round, and put it back on again.... The baby cow elephant was lying in the narrow barrier-moat on her back, her legs up to the sky. She had suffered severe stomach injuries and could not move.

Three hippopotamuses were drowned when iron debris pinned them to the bottom of their water basin. In the ape house, Sailer-Jackson found a gibbon that, when it reached out to the trainer, had no hands, only stumps. "Haunted by the expression of suffering on its face," McKee writes, "[the trainer] drew his pistol and shot the beast." A badly burned female polar bear tried to protect her cubs by covering them. She was also shot but, since there was no milk in the ruins of Dresden, the cubs died of hunger within days. Nearly forty rhesus monkeys escaped to the trees but were dead by the next day from drinking water polluted by the incendiary chemicals. For those animals who made it to the next day, the assault was far from over.

A U.S. aircraft pilot came in low, firing at anything he could see that was still alive. "In this way," Sailer-Jackson explained, "our last giraffe met her death. Many stags and others animals which we had managed to save, became victims of this hero."[13]

In his wartime memoirs, Winston Churchill seemed unable to work up much emotion in recalling the Dresden assault. "We made a heavy raid in the latter month on Dresden," he wrote, "then a centre of communication of Germany's Eastern Front."[14]

DEATH FROM ABOVE (PART TWO)

In the Pacific theater, Bomber Harris would have been no match for American General Curtis LeMay, head of the Twenty-first Bomber Command. Acting upon Marshall's 1941 idea of torching the poorer areas of Japan's cities, on the night of March 9-10, 1945, LeMay's bombers laid siege on Tokyo, where tightly-packed wooden buildings were assaulted by 1,665 tons of incendiaries. LeMay later recalled that a few explosives had been mixed in with the incendiaries to demoralize fire-fighters (96 fire engines burned to ashes and 88 firemen died).[15]

One Japanese doctor recalled "countless bodies" floating in the

Sumida River. These bodies were "as black as charcoal" and indistinguishable as men or women. The total dead for one night was an estimated 85,000, with 40,000 injured and one million left homeless. This was only the first strike in a firebombing campaign that dropped 250 tons of bombs per square mile, destroying 40 percent of the surface area in 66 death-list cities (including Hiroshima and Nagasaki). The attack area was 87.4 percent residential.[16]

It is believed that more people died from fire in a six-hour time period than ever before in the history of mankind. At ground zero, the temperature reached 1,800° Fahrenheit. Flames from the ensuing inferno were visible for 200 miles. Due to the intense heat, canals boiled over, metals melted, and human beings burst spontaneously into flames.

By May 1945, 75 percent of the bombs being dropped on Japan were incendiaries. Cheered on by the likes of *Time* magazine—who explained that "properly kindled, Japanese cities will burn like autumn leaves"—LeMay's campaign took an estimated 672,000 lives.[17]

Radio Tokyo termed LeMay's tactics "slaughter bombing" and the Japanese press declared that through the fire raids:

> America has revealed her barbaric character.... It was an attempt at mass murder of women and children.... The action of the Americans is all the more despicable because of the noisy pretensions they constantly make about their humanity and idealism.... No one expects war to be anything but a brutal business, but it remains for the Americans to make it systematically and unnecessarily a wholesale horror for innocent victims.[18]

Rather than denying this, a spokesman for the Fifth Air Force categorized "the entire population of Japan [as] a proper military target." Colonel Harry F. Cunningham explained the U.S. policy in no uncertain terms:

> We military men do not pull punches or put on Sunday
> School picnics. We are making War and making it in the
> all-out fashion which saves American lives, shortens the
> agony which War is and seeks to bring about an enduring
> Peace. We intend to seek out and destroy the enemy wher-
> ever he or she is, in the greatest possible numbers, in the
> shortest possible time. For us, THERE ARE NO CIVIL-
> IANS IN JAPAN.[19]

On the morning of August 6, 1945, before the Hiroshima story
broke, a page-one headline in the *Atlanta Constitution* read: 580
B-29s RAIN FIRE ON 4 MORE DEATH-LIST CITIES. Ironically, the
success of LeMay's firebombing raids had effectively eliminated
Tokyo from the list of possible A-bomb targets—as there was
nothing left to bomb.

REGRETS, THEY HAD A FEW

Not all U.S. military cheered the incendiary policy in the Pacific.
In a confidential memo of June 1945, Brigadier General Bonner
Fellers, an aide to MacArthur, called the raids, "one of the most
ruthless and barbaric killings on non-combatants in all history."[20]

Secretary of War Henry Stimson recorded that it was
"appalling that there had been no protest over the air strikes we
were conducting against Japan which led to such extraordinarily
heavy loss of life." Stimson added that he thought "there was
something wrong with a country where no one questioned that,"[21]
before telling President Truman that the saturation bombing of
Japan concerned him for two reasons:

"First," he began, "because I did not want to have the United
States get the reputation for outdoing Hitler in atrocities."

Before getting too carried away with his noble rhetoric,
Stimson quickly added that his second reason for concern was that
he was "fearful that before we could get ready, the Air Force might
have Japan so thoroughly bombed out that the new weapon [read:

atomic bomb] would not have a fair background to show its strength."[22]

The ultimate Allied war crimes—Hiroshima and Nagasaki—are discussed next in Chapter Six.

DAM AND GRAHAM

When investigating Allied war crimes during WWII, it is informative to note that of the 185 Nazis indicted at Nuremberg, only twenty-four were sentenced to death, one of whom was the German High Commissioner in Holland. His crime? Ordering the opening of Dutch dikes to slow the advance of Allied troops. Roughly 500,000 acres were flooded and the result was mass starvation.

In pondering the good vs. evil WWII dichotomy, one might consider that the United States Air Force, fresh from fighting the forces of evil, bombed the Toksan Dam (among others) during the Korean War in order to flood North Korea's rice farms. Here's how the USAF justified such tactics:

> To the Communists the smashing of the dams meant primarily the destruction of their chief sustenance—rice. The Westerner can little conceive the awesome meaning that the loss of this staple food commodity has for an Asian—starvation and slow death.

This dam-bombing/people-starving technique, culled from the wartime strategy of one of Hitler's twenty-four best and brightest, continued right on into Vietnam—with orders coming directly from the top, so to speak.

In a now-declassified memorandum dated April 15, 1969, evangelist Billy Graham, having just returned from meeting missionaries in Bangkok, gave his approval to a plan that could potentially drown thousands and starve many more; the holy man urged President Nixon to blow up dikes "which could overnight destroy the economy of North Vietnam." With or without Rev. Graham's sanction, U.S. bombing of dikes in South Vietnam was already a common and uncontroversial tactic.[23]

CRUEL AND UNUSUAL

While the treatment of Japanese prisoners of war was commonly little more than making sure there were not any Japanese prisoners of war, those Axis soldiers captured in the European theater often learned firsthand how good the good guys were.

Adams tells of U.S. policies toward taking prisoners:

Before the invasion of Sicily, General Patton told his men to accept no surrender from enemy soldiers who continued to fire within the highly lethal 200-yards range. At Biscari, U.S. troops killed thirty-four unarmed prisoners who had given up at the correct distance, but these GIs had seen buddies killed, and they didn't feel that a few yards made any difference.... [Even] Audie Murphy told new men to take no prisoners and to kill Axis wounded.

Many of those who were actually taken prisoner may have soon wished they were killed.

"Captured Germans held in France under the command of General Dwight D. Eisenhower were systematically starved," writes David K. Wright[24] while another 676,000 or so German prisoners were shipped to the United States between 1942 and 1946.[25]

"In U.S. camps," agrees Cockburn, "POWs were starved to the point of collapse, performed 20 million man-days of work on army posts and 10 million man-days for contract employers. Some were assigned to work for the Chemical Warfare Center at Edgewood Arsenal in Maryland."[26]

Some 372,000 German POWs in the United States were

forced—at the behest of Eleanor Roosevelt—to undergo a re-education program, "to return them to 'Christian practices' and to reject 'German thinking,' says Cockburn. "As time wore on, the name of the program was changed to 'intellectual diversion'."

Canadian writer James Bacque, in his book *Other Losses*, goes even further, claiming that up to one million German POWs in Europe died from Allied neglect while others were used by the French to fight the Vietnamese. While perusing "Good War" documents called the "Weekly Prisoner of War and Disarmed Enemy Report," Bacque found statistics under the heading "Other Losses" which he interpreted to mean POW deaths. The author consulted with Colonel Philip S. Lauben, who had been chief of the German Affairs Branch of the Supreme Headquarters, Allied Expeditionary Force (SHAEF).

"[Other Losses] means deaths and escapes," Lauben explained.

When asked how many escapes he recalled, Lauben replied, "Very, very minor." Bacque later discovered the number was less than one-tenth of one percent.

"It is beyond doubt," Bacque writes, "that enormous numbers of men of all ages, plus some women and children, died of exposure, unsanitary conditions, disease and starvation in the American and French camps in Germany and France starting in April 1945." Bacque puts those numbers at "almost certainly over 900,000, and quite likely over a million."[27]

Needless to say, these controversial figures have been vigorously denied by official sources. Michael C.C. Adams addressed Bacque's unsettling work in his book:

Bacques' credibility has been assailed by Stephen Ambrose, a biographer of Dwight D. Eisenhower, the man who would bear ultimate responsibility for these crimes. Ambrose points out that Bacque at times relied on slender or circumstantial evidence and that it would have been hard to keep so great a scandal quiet for so long [*New York Times Book Review*, February 24, 1991]. On the other hand, American guards have come forward to support Bacque. One wrote: 'I witnessed the atrocities Stephen E. Ambrose tries to deny or gloss over' [*New York Times Book Review*, April 14, 1991].... The truth is probably somewhere in the middle.... As another guard admitted: 'we sometimes slipped over the boundary of civilized behavior and resembled to some extent what we were fighting against.'

With the high level of censorship existing in the Allied theater of operations, perhaps the key to keeping "so great a scandal quiet for so long" is that, for most people, it never existed. At the time, General George S. Patton wrote in his diary: "Ike made the sensational statement that while hostilities were in progress, the one important thing was order and discipline, but now that hostilities were over, the important thing was to stay in with world public opinion—apparently whether it was right or wrong.... Eisenhower talked to us very confidentially on the necessity for solidarity in the event that any of us are called before a Congressional Committee."[28]

PAINT THE TOWN BLACK

"At the core," writes U.S. apologist, Stephen E. Ambrose, "the American citizen soldiers knew the difference between right and wrong, and they didn't want to live in a world in which wrong prevailed."[29] To believe this and further perpetrate the "Good War" myth, Ambrose must ignore, among many other things, the issue of AWOL American soldiers running wild in Europe.

"Paris was full of them," remarks Adams in *The Best War Ever*. Chet Antonine has written of U.S. troops "looting the German city of Jena where the famous Zeiss company made the best cameras in the world." According to Antonine, the U.S. compiled a list of "Continental AWOLs" that included as many as 50,000 men. Many of them turned to the black market.[30]

"Allied soldiers [in Italy] stole from the populace and the government, and once, GIs stole a trainload of sugar, complete with the engine," writes Adams.

V.S. Pritchett, in the April 7, 1945 *New Statesman and Nation*, wrote about GIs stealing cameras, motorbikes, wine glasses, and books. In the *New York Herald Tribune*, John Steinbeck reported on three soldiers arrested for selling stolen watches. In October 1945 alone, American GIs sent home $5,470,777 more than they were paid.[31]

One illegal form of currency for GIs—AWOL or otherwise—was whiskey. As alcohol dependency rose, desperate soldiers resorted to such homegrown brews as Aqua Velva and grapefruit juice or medical alcohol blended with torpedo fluid.

The buying and trading wasn't limited to moonshine. Throughout the European theater of operations, the Allied soldiers did their best to promote the world's oldest profession.

"In a ruined world where a pack of cigarettes sold for $100 American, GIs were millionaires," says Antonine. "A candy bar bought sex from nearly any starving German girl."

"Soldiers had sex, wherever and whenever possible," Adams reports. "Seventy-five percent of GIs overseas, whether married or not, admitted to having intercourse. Unchanneled sexual need produced rape, occasionally even murder. Away from home, where nobody knew them, some GIs forced themselves on women." In northern Europe, venereal disease (VD) caused more U.S. casualties than the German V-2 rocket. In France, the VD rate rose 600 percent after the liberation of Paris.

Where did those 50,000 AWOL GIs go after doing their part to soil the image of a good war? Nearly three thousand were court-martialed[32] and one, Private Eddie Slovik (of G Company, 109th Infantry Regiment, 28th Infantry Division) was executed. The Detroit native deserted in August 1944, surrendered in October of that same year, and was put on trial a month later. General Eisenhower signed the execution order of December 23, 1944, and Slovik faced a twelve-man firing squad at St. Marie aux Mines in eastern France shortly thereafter. None of the eleven bullets (one is always a blank) struck the intended target—Slovik's heart—and it was a full three minutes before he died.[33] Outrage spread quickly and there were no further executions.

As for the rest of the AWOL GIs, Chet Antonine's guess seems as good as any: "A goodly number of them undoubtedly stayed on in Europe as they had [after] World War One. Perhaps some of them got bogged down in ordinary life, marrying and having children. Others may have continued their lives of crime and ended up in prison. Only nine thousand of them had been found by 1948."

A PORTRAIT OF A WAR CRIMINAL AS A YOUNG MAN

As reported by Antonine, there was a certain staff sergeant who used his authority to "become absolute lord of the [German] town of Bensheim" during those black market days, future Nobel Peace Prize winner, Henry Kissinger.

"After evicting the owners from their villa," Antonine writes, "Kissinger moved in with his German girlfriend, maid, housekeeper, and secretary and began to throw fancy parties."

These fancy parties were not the norm in Bensheim, an area where the average German made due on a daily food intake of fewer than 850 calories—that's less food than was given to prisoners at the Bergen-Belsen concentration camp.

Staff Sergeant Kissinger's post-war compassion was subsequently displayed throughout his tenure as a high-ranking U.S. government official. His role in repression and state-sponsored murder is well-documented from Southeast Asia to Bangladesh to East Timor to Chile. After the 1998 arrest of Chilean General Augusto Pinochet in Britain, Ken Silverstein and Alexander Cockburn pondered:

If there is truly justice in the world then, the next time Henry Kissinger steps onto foreign soil, there will be a warrant seeking his arrest and his extradition. It was, after all, Kissinger, as Secretary of State, who stated that the Chilean people should not be permitted the irresponsibility of electing [Salvador] Allende.... And if not extradition to Chile, then why not kindred extradition orders for Kissinger from Cambodia, or Laos or Vietnam or any of the other nations where torturers, death squads, and military goons were pressed into action by this man, when he was the prime executive of U.S. foreign policy?[34]

But then again, as Kissinger himself has remarked, "Foreign policy should not be confused with missionary work."[35]

NOTES FOR CHAPTER FIVE

1. Udall, Stewart. *Myths of August* (New York: Pantheon Books, 1994) p. 52
2. Udall, p. 51
3. Cockburn, p. 191
4. McKee, Alexander *Dresden 1945: The Devil's Tinderbox* (New York: Dutton, 1984) pp. 64-5
5. Cockburn, p. 301
6. Udall, p. 55
7. Adams, p. 54
8. Fussell, p. 17-8
9. Fussell, p. 23
10. McKee, p. 45
11. McKee, p. 46
12. McKee, p. 47
13. McKee, pp. 78-9; 193-6; 222-3
14. Zinn, p. 408. A fine illustration of life in a propaganda state presented itself in mid-1995. With much of the Western world paralyzed by spasms of fifty-years-since-the-end-of-WWII anniversaries, the *New York Times* got into the act with a piece entitled, "The Rebirth of Dresden Brings a Tourist Boom." (July 16, 1995; p. 3 of the travel section) Announcing that "few cities in Europe are pulsating like Dresden," reporter Steven Kinzer trumpeted the rebuilding of the eighteenth century Church of Our Lady "with the help of sponsors from around the world, including a group of British pilots who took part in the air raids." British and American allies are making their presence felt in Dresden ("Once known as Florence on the Elbe," Kinzer reminds us), only now they're spending upwards of $207 per night at the Treff-Hotel for a riverview. And this time around, as the *Times* details, the exact number of people hitting town is no mystery—rising from 464,896 tourists in 1992 to 662,742 in 1994 (a number that has probably grown since then, thanks to Kinzer and the *Times*). Did the American "newspaper of record" inject any political reference into what appeared to be a verbatim reprint of a Dresden Chamber of Commerce press release? Stephen Kinzer was careful to note that while the reconstruction of the once-devastated city began during the days of Communist rule, "only recently has a true boom begun." Now we know what those forty-five years of tension and trillions of dollars of expenditures during the Cold War were all

about.

15. Adams, p. 54

16. Shalom, p. 77

17. Adams, p. 66

18. Edoin, Hoito. *The Night Tokyo Burned* (New York: St. Martin's Press, 1987) p. 120

19. Takaki, pp. 28-9

20. Shalom, p. 77

21. Cockburn, p. 249

22. Shalom, p. 77

23. Cockburn, pp. 99-100

24. D. Wright, p. 70

25. M. Wright, p. 185

26. Cockburn, p. 195

27. James Bacque. *Other Losses: The Shocking Truth Behind the Mass Deaths of Disarmed German Soldiers and Civilians Under General Eisenhower's Command* (Rocklin, CA: Prima Publishing, 1991) pp. 1-2. A more widely accepted number for German POWs who died while in U.S. custody is 56,000—mostly from malnutrition. When food shortages developed, Eisenhower reclassified POWS as DEFs (Disarmed Enemy Forces) thereby exempting the German prisoners from the minimum standard of care for POWs as prescribed by the Geneva Convention.

28. Bacque, p. 149

29. Stephen E. Ambrose. *Citizen Soldiers: The U.S. Army from the Normandy Beaches to the Bulge to the Surrender of Germany, June 7, 1944 to May 7, 1945* (New York: Touchstone, 1997) p. 473

30. Chet Antonine. "Johnny Sold His Gun: The Untold Story of U.S. Outlaw GIs in WWII Europe," *Loompanics Main Catalog* (Loompanics Unlimited books), 1992, p. 2

31. Antonine, p. 3

32. Antonine, p. 6 (for all remaining Antonine quotes in this chapter)

33. Polmar, Norman and Allen, Thomas B. *World War II: The Encyclopedia of the War Years, 1941-1945* (New York: Random House, 1996) pp. 737-9

34. Cockburn, Alexander and Silverstein, Ken. "Pinochet and the U.S.," *CounterPunch*, Dec. 1-15, 1998, p. 3

35. Hitchens, p. 253

CHAPTER SIX

"We've Got the Cards..."

"It is an atomic bomb...It is the greatest thing in history."

—President Harry S. Truman,
August 6, 1945

A s we contemplate a new century that will bring us bio-engineered and genetically-altered foodstuffs (and per-haps even human organs and organisms), it's illuminat-ing to spend some time examining the great technological innova-tion of the twentieth century: nuclear power. Born amidst the mur-derous madness of WWII, the atomic industry (and its benefactors in the Pentagon) stand as the cautionary tale to end all cautionary tales. The much-hyped atom has evolved into a nefarious nuclear nightmare, another corporate reality unrecognized in a nation built on denial and delusion.

At first, in 1945, the supposed war-ending ability of atomic energy caused Senator Brien McMahon of Connecticut to gush that it was "the most important thing in history since the birth of Jesus Christ."[1] Slightly more than half a century later, David Lilienthal, physicist, Nobel Prize winner, and the first chairman of the U.S. Atomic Energy Commission, saw things a little differently:

Once a bright hope shared by all mankind, including myself, the rash proliferation of nuclear power plants is now one of the ugliest clouds hanging over America.[2]

The journey from Second Coming to second thoughts commenced during the Second World War. Its was baptized in the blood of 210,000 Japanese citizens[3]—not to mention the U.S. POWs stationed near the doomed cities. The death count across the globe in the ensuing decades is incalculable, whether it be from direct radiation poisoning, the use of nuclear medicine, the diversion of funds to support the arms race, or the sadly predictable power plant accidents. Today, with the problem of reprocessing, recycling, or storing nuclear wastes looming on the horizon, it is nearly impossible to assess the extent of the future damage that will be wrought from the radioactive flames of Hiroshima and Nagasaki.

Why was the bomb used? The myths abound. The most common answer is that President Truman ordered the attack, as Professor Perry puts it (in the single paragraph he dedicates to the premeditated nuking of civilians), "to avoid an American invasion of the Japanese homeland, which would have cost hundreds of thousands of lives." Is this rationale accurate?

BLAME IT ON ADOLF

Before confronting Truman's alleged reasoning for unleashing the bomb, there is another, lesser-known myth surrounding the Manhattan Project that must be dealt with: the life-and-death race with Hitler and the Nazi scientists he had working on an atomic program of their own. "Working at Los Alamos, New Mexico, under the direction of J. Robert Oppenheimer," writes historian Kenneth C. Davis, "atomic scientists, many of them refugees from Hitler's Europe, thought they were racing against Germans developing a 'Nazi bomb.'"[4]

Surely, if it was possible for the epitome of evil to produce such a weapon, it would be the responsibility of the good guys to beat *der Führer* to the plutonium punch. While such a desperate race makes for excellent melodrama, it bears more resemblance to the never-ending supply of arms "gaps" produced by Cold War propagandists than to reality.

The German bomb effort, however, fell far short of success[5]

Thanks to the declassification of key documents, we now have access to "unassailable proof that the race with the Nazis was a fiction," says Stewart Udall, who cites the work of McGeorge Bundy and Thomas Powers before adding that, "According to the official history of the British Secret Intelligence Service (SIS), those agents maintained 'contacts with scientists in neutral countries…'" These contacts, by mid-1943, provided enough evidence to convince the SIS that the German bomb program simply did not exist.[6]

Despite such findings, U.S. General Leslie Groves, military commander of the Manhattan Project, got permission in the fall of 1943 to begin a secret espionage mission known as *Alsos* (a name chosen by Groves, Greek for "grove"). The mission saw Groves's men following the Allies' armies throughout Europe with the goal of capturing German scientists involved in the manufacture of atomic weapons.[7]

While the data uncovered by *Alsos* only served to reinforce the prior reports that the Third Reich was not pursuing a nuclear program, Groves (with the help of Secretary of War Stimson) was able to maintain enough of a cover-up to keep his pet project alive. The criminal concealment of the truth about the Nazis and their lack of atomic research kept the momentum going in the New Mexico desert and, "swept it, following Germany's defeat, onto a path that led to Hiroshima and to the creation of misinformation that has obscured essential truths concerning the Manhattan Project and the epoch it initiated."[8]

In the no-holds-barred religion of anti-communism, the "Good War" enemy was never fascism. Truman's daughter, Margaret, remarked about her dad's early presidential efforts after the death of FDR in April 1945, "My father's overriding concern in these first weeks was our policy towards Russia."[9]

THE INVASION THAT NEVER WAS

The most commonly evoked justification for the dropping of atomic bombs on Japan was to save lives, but even Marvin Perry admits, "Truman's decision has aroused considerable debate. Some analysts maintain that dropping the bomb was unnecessary." Perry even goes as far as daring to inform his readers that since Stalin was about to send the Red Army at the withering Empire of Japan, "it has been suggested that Truman wanted to end the war immediately, thus depriving the U.S.S.R. of an opportunity to extend its influence in East Asia." However, this prospect remains essentially unexamined in his textbook except for a timetable that shows Russia entering the war against Japan two days *after* Hiroshima.

Other historians and analysts have delved deeper. Was it true that an Allied invasion of the Japanese homeland would have cost many lives? Would such an invasion even have been necessary? Finally, were the actions of the United States motivated by an escalating Cold War with the Soviet Union? Volumes have been written attempting to answer these questions. Here are the facts that don't mesh with the long-accepted storyline:

Although hundreds of thousands of Japanese lives were lost in Hiroshima and Nagasaki, the bombings are often explained away as a life-saving measure—American lives. Exactly how many lives were saved is, however, up for grabs. (We do know of a few U.S. soldiers who fell between the cracks. About a dozen or more American POWs were killed in Hiroshima, a truth that remained hidden for some 30 years.)[10]

In defense of the U.S. action, it is usually claimed that the bombs saved lives. The hypothetical body count ranges from 20,000 to 1.2 million.[11]

In an August 9, 1945 statement to "the men and women of the Manhattan Project," President Truman declared the hope that "this new weapon will result in saving thousands of American lives."[12]

"The president's initial formulation of 'thousands,' however, was clearly not his final statement on the matter to say the least," remarks historian Gar Alperovitz. In fact, in his book, *The Decision to Use the Atomic Bomb and the Architecture of an American Myth,* Alperovitz documents but a few of Truman's public estimates throughout the years:

- December 15, 1945: "It occurred to me that a quarter of a million of the flower of our young manhood was worth a couple of Japanese cities..."
- Late 1946: "A year less of war will mean life for three hundred thousand—maybe half a million—of America's finest youth."
- October 1948: "...in the long run we could save a quarter of a million young Americans from being killed, and would save an equal number of Japanese young men from being killed."
- April 6, 1949: "...I thought 200,000 of our young men would be saved. . ."
- November 1949: Truman quotes Army Chief of Staff George C. Marshall as estimating the cost of an Allied invasion of Japan to be "half a million casualties."
- January 12, 1953: Still quoting Marshall, Truman raises the estimate to "a minimum one quarter of a million" and maybe "as much as a million, on the American side alone, with an equal number of the enemy."
- Finally, on April 28, 1959, Truman concluded: "the dropping of the bombs...saved millions of lives."[13]

Winston Churchill proclaimed that the Allies "now had something in [their] hands which would redress the balance with the Russians." He topped Truman's ceiling by exclaiming how those A-bombs spared well over 1.2 million Allied lives.[14]

Fortunately, we are not operating without the benefit of official estimates.

In June of 1945, President Truman ordered the U.S. military to calculate the cost in American lives for a planned assault on Japan. Consequently, the Joint War Plans Committee prepared a report for the Chiefs of Staff, dated June 15, 1945, thus providing the closest thing anyone has to "accurate": 40,000 U.S. soldiers killed, 150,000 wounded, and 3,500 missing.[15]

While the actual casualty count remains unknowable, it was widely known at the time that Japan had been trying to surrender for months prior to the atomic bombing. A May 5, 1945 cable, intercepted and decoded by the U.S. "dispelled any possible doubt that the Japanese were eager to sue for peace."[16] In fact, the United States Strategic Bombing Survey reported, shortly after the war, that Japan "in all probability" would have surrendered *before* the much-discussed November 1, 1945 Allied invasion of the homeland, thereby saving all kinds of lives.[17]

Truman himself eloquently noted in his diary that Stalin would "be in the Jap War on August 15th. Fini *(sic)* Japs when that comes about."[18]

Clearly, Truman saw the bombs as way to end the war before the Soviet Union could claim a major role in Japan's terms of surrender. However, one year after Hiroshima and Nagasaki, a top-secret U.S. study concluded that the Japanese surrender was based more upon Stalin's declaration of war than either of the atomic bombs.[19]

Many post-Hiroshima/Nagasaki sentiments questioned the use of the bombs.

"I thought our country should avoid shocking world opinion by the use of a weapon whose employment was, I thought, no longer mandatory as a measure to save American lives," said General Dwight D. Eisenhower[20] while, not long after the Japanese surrender, *New York Times* military analyst Hanson Baldwin wrote, "The enemy, in a military sense, was in a hopeless strategic position...."

Such then, was the situation when we wiped out Hiroshima and Nagasaki. Need we have done it? No one can, of course, be positive, but the answer is almost certainly negative."[21]

Was it the cold logic of capitalism that motivated the nuking of civilians? As far back as May 1945, a Venezuelan diplomat was reporting how Assistant Secretary of State Nelson Rockefeller "communicated to us the anxiety of the United States government about the Russian attitude."[22] U.S. Secretary of State James F. Byrnes seemed to agree when he turned the anxiety up a notch by explaining how "our possessing and demonstrating the bomb would make Russia more manageable in the East.... The demonstration of the bomb might impress Russia with America's military might."[23]

General Leslie Groves, military commander of the Manhattan Project, was less cryptic:

> There was never, from about two weeks from the time I took charge of this Project, any illusion on my part but that Russia was our enemy, and the Project was conducted on that basis."[24]

During the same time period, President Truman noted that Secretary of War Henry Stimson was "at least as much concerned with the role of the atomic bomb in the shaping of history as in its capacity to shorten the war." What sort of shaping Stimson had in mind might be discerned from his September 11, 1945 comment to the president: "I consider the problem of our satisfactory relations with Russia as not merely connected but as virtually dominated by the problem of the atomic bomb."[25]

Stimson called the bomb a "diplomatic weapon," and duly explained that "American statesmen were eager for their country to browbeat the Russians with the bomb held rather ostentatiously on our hip."[26]

"By late 1945," adds Davis, "it was clear to Truman and other American leaders that victory over Germany and Japan would not mean peace. Stalin's intention to create a buffer of socialist states surrounding the Soviet Union and under the control of the Red Army was already apparent. Atomic muscle-flexing may have been the overriding consideration in Truman's decision."[27] Noam Chomsky concurs:

"It's very likely that a large part of the motive in the atom bombing was to cut off the possibility of Russian participation in control of East Asia," he told David Barsamian in a 1995 interview. "The U.S. took a very strong line on that. We not only kept the Russians out, we kept the British and the French and the Dutch and everyone out. The Far Eastern Commission, which was supposed to oversee Japanese affairs, the U.S. ruled with an iron hand. They wouldn't let anyone in…. You can debate exactly the extent to which the atom bomb was motivated by those considerations, but it was certainly not trivial."

Neither was the intended impact of the atom bombs on America's enemies trivial.

"The psychological effect on Stalin was twofold," proposes Charles L. Mee, Jr. "The Americans had not only used a doomsday machine; they had used it when, as Stalin knew, it was not militarily necessary. It was this last chilling fact that doubtless made the greatest impression on the Russians."[28]

Imagine the impression it made on the citizens of Hiroshima and Nagasaki.

"Why did we drop [the bomb]?" pondered Studs Terkel at the time of the fiftieth anniversary of the Hiroshima and Nagasaki bombings. "So little Harry could show Molotov and Stalin we've got the cards. That was the phrase Truman used. We showed the goddamned Russians we've got something and they'd better behave themselves in Europe. That's why it was dropped. The evidence is overwhelming. And yet you tell that to 99 percent of Americans and they'll spit in your eye."[29]

GROUND ZERO

According to the August 15, 1945 edition of the *New York Daily News*, 60 percent of Hiroshima—a city with a population of roughly 343,000—was destroyed by the bomb. A Tokyo radio broadcast on August 8 described how "the impact of the bomb was so terrific that practically all living things, human and animal, were seared to death by the tremendous heat and pressure engendered by the blast."

Tokyo radio went on to call Hiroshima a city with corpses "too numerous to be counted...literally seared to death." It was impossible to "distinguish between men and women." The Associated Press carried the first eye-witness account: a Japanese soldier who described the victims as "bloated and scorched—such an awesome sight—their legs and bodies stripped of clothes and burned with a huge blister..."[30]

A Japanese wire service added, "Many of those who received burns cannot survive the wounds because of the uncanny effects which the atomic bomb produces on the human body. Even those who received minor burns, and looked quite healthy at first, weakened after a few days for some unknown reason." U.S. officials deemed this type of report the work of Japanese propaganda, calling them "abstract" theories attempting to "capitalize on the horror of the atomic bombing in an effort to win sympathy from their conquerors,"[31] but the work of Australian war correspondent, Wilfred Burchett, reporting from Tokyo on September 2, 1945, cannot be so glibly dismissed.

After visiting the devastated city, Burchett described Hiroshima as a "death-stricken alien planet" with patients presenting purple skin hemorrhages, hair loss, drastically reduced white blood cell counts, fever, nausea, gangrene, and other symptoms of a radiation disease he called an "atomic plague." His findings were initially challenged by U.S. officials, of course, but when Burchett himself ended up in the hospital with a abnormally low white blood cell count, such challenges lost some of their impact.[32]

Official response to the mass murder was mixed, but for every Canadian Prime Minister Mackenzie King who, after the bombing, "expressed his relief that the bomb had been dropped on Asiatic people, not on the 'white races' of Europe,"[33] there was a Herbert Hoover, who declared on September 27, 1945:

> Despite any sophistries, [the bomb's] major use is not to kill fighting men, but to kill women, children, and civilian men of whole cities as a pressure on governments. If it comes into general use, we may see all civilization destroyed.[34]

African-American novelist Zora Neale Hurston called Truman a "monster," adding, "I can think of him as nothing else but the Butcher of Asia," and even Admiral William D. Leahy characterized the atom bombs as "an inhuman weapon to use on a people that was already defeated and ready to surrender."

Life magazine summed up Allied bombing tactics during WWII in its August 1945 issue.

> From the very concept of strategic bombing, all the developments—night, pattern, saturation, area, indiscriminate— have led straight to Hiroshima, and Hiroshima was, and was intended to be, almost pure *Schrecklichkeit* [terror bombing].

At 11 o'clock in the morning of August 9, Prime Minister Kintaro Suzuki told the Japanese Cabinet that Japan's "only alternative" was to accept the Allied peace terms and "terminate the war."

Minutes later, the second bomb fell on Nagasaki.[35]

If Hiroshima was pure *Schrecklichkeit*, who then could explain the purpose of Nagasaki? Here are the thoughts of some who have tried:

"The bombing of Nagasaki had even less military justification than that of Hiroshima," says Shalom. "Two days after the first bomb, Moscow declared war on Japan.... [Army Chief of Staff] George C. Marshall ordered a crash propaganda campaign to inform the Japanese public about the bomb in order to get them to press for surrender. Propaganda leaflets were dropped on many cities, but Nagasaki did not get its full quota of leaflets until August 10, the day after it was obliterated."[36]

"The dropping of the second bomb on Nagasaki seems to have been scheduled in advance and no one has ever explained why it was dropped," Howard Zinn writes. "Was it because this was a plutonium bomb whereas the Hiroshima bomb was a uranium bomb? Were the dead and irradiated of Nagasaki victim of a scientific experiment?"[37]

"Humanity had been forced to witness enormous destruction all through World War II," declares historian Michael C.C. Adams, in an attempt to understand the use of atom bombs and the relative lack of outrage afterwards. "By 1945, the killing had reached such enormous proportions that the bombing of one more city did not have the aspect of moral horror that it might have now. In such a time of death, the unimaginable had become acceptable."[38]

I'LL TAKE MANHATTAN

The men who helped make the unimaginable acceptable toiled at Los Alamos, New Mexico while U.S. propagandists worked overtime to prepare the world for the coming nuclear age. The scientific director at Los Alamos was J. Robert Oppenheimer, a man who, in 1943, pioneered the idea of "poisoning the German food supply with radioactive strontium."

"We should not attempt a plan," Oppenheimer explained to his boss, General Leslie Groves, "unless we can poison food sufficient to kill half a million men."[39] Within a few years, however, Oppenheimer began to see things a little differently.

After learning of the horrors his bomb had wrought on Japan, the scientist began to harbor second thoughts, and he resigned in October 1945. In March of the following year, Oppenheimer told Truman:

"Mr. President, I have blood on my hands."

Truman's reply?

"It'll come out in the wash."

Later, the president told an aide, "Don't bring that fellow around again."[40]

For others at Los Alamos, life (and death) went on. In the case of Louis Slotin, a thirty-four-year-old Canadian physicist, his work would bring home the experience of Hiroshima and Nagasaki:

> While other scientists watched in tense silence, Slotin delicately manipulated a screwdriver barely separating two silvery-gray globes of fissionable plutonium. One time, he slipped, the globes touched, and radiation flooded the laboratory. Slotin lunged forward and pushed the plutonium apart, saving the others. His own dosage of radiation, he knew, was lethal; with chalk, he marked the positions of others in the room and calculated on a nearby blackboard that they would live. Then he became nauseated. His arms, legs, and face swelled hideously. Within a week, he became incoherent and died.[41]

As Oppenheimer and Slotin each suffered from their involvement with the "Good War" and its progeny, the burgeoning nuclear industry, the world of public relations was hard at work making sure the general public's perception of the mighty atom would ensure a steady supply of tax dollars for decades to come. Between 1940 and 1998, the total amount of money, in constant 1996 dollars, spent by the U.S. on nuclear weapons and weapons-related programs was nearly $5.5 trillion.[42]

Censorship first reared its ugly head when General Groves chose a press pool of one to cover the Manhattan Project: William L. Laurence of the *New York Times*, the paper's science reporter since 1930. Spinning stories of the "atom's redemptive role," Laurence found the nuclear research "comparable only with the biblical genesis."[43] Thus, the average American's first exposure to radiation was, in a way, no less damaging than those to come.

President Eisenhower's now-famous "Atoms for Peace" speech to the United Nations in 1953 marked the beginning of a full-blown campaign (spear-headed by Laurence) to promote the use of nuclear energy, which would eventually provide electricity "too cheap to meter," went the thinking of the day.

Despite the tragic litany of accidents, leaks, spills, and deaths, the PR machine continues to churn on today—to the point where nuclear conglomerates like Westinghouse and General Electric actually own television and radio networks and mainstream commentators play right into the myth.

"[The American GIs] had seen enough killing; they wanted to save lives," writes Stephen E. Ambrose. "They licked polio and made other revolutionary advances in medicine."[44] Thanks to such propaganda, the image of radiation has gone from destroyer of lives to "medicine."

EVERY FAMILY IS A NUCLEAR FAMILY

To demonstrate the shameful legacy of the U.S. nuclear industry, post-Hiroshima and Nagasaki, let's look at the Hanford Reservation in Washington state, where the plutonium for the Nagasaki bomb was created in 1943.

Thanks to poor planning, says noted activist and author Dr. Helen Caldicott, sixty percent (by volume) of the nation's highly radioactive, dissolved high-level waste from reactor fuel is now stored in "corrosive-prone, single-walled, one-million gallon carbon steel tanks sunk in the desert floor." Sixty-six of the 149 tanks have leaked and at least 750,000 gallons of liquid high-level waste have entered the surrounding soil. As a result of this and other leaks (including those from the six Polaris submarines buried at Hanford and the irradiated fuel sent there from Three Mile Island), the nearby Columbia River is being fed by ground water contaminated with uranium, strontium 90, iodine 129, and plutonium.

"In fact," says Caldicott, "this beautiful river has been designated one of the most radioactive in the world, yet people still catch and eat fish without protection or warnings about health dangers."

Hanford is described now by Caldicott as "America's nuclear cemetery—a vast dead satanic area, poisonous for millions of years."[45]

The testing of the technology needed to annihilate two Japanese cities took place in the continental United States and the subsequent fallout has created a new breed of American: the downwinder.

Documentarian and photographer Carole Gallagher is the author of *American Ground Zero: The Secret Nuclear War*. In her book, she serves up an oral history of those Americans who experienced the fallout from the many atomic and hydrogen bombs exploded in the United States, including 126 tests at the Nevada Test Site.

"[The map] makes very clear that the entire state of Utah was seriously irradiated along with most of the other Western states," Gallagher explains, "but the radiation was also carried by winds to the Northeast, all over the U.S. in fact." One Air Force colonel who monitored nuclear fallout throughout the U.S., Canada, and Mexico told Gallagher, "We are all downwinders."

"I do not know where we found the arrogance to call the Soviet Union 'the Evil Empire,'" Gallagher declares, "but I do recall the words of the town mortician in St. George, Utah, who used to embalm the tiny wasted bodies of children who had died from leukemia: 'They done to us what the Russians couldn't do.'"[46]

For any American who has somehow managed to elude the irradiated winds of war, NASA has cooked up a scheme that should strike fear into anyone whose immune system has not yet been compromised: nukes in space.

The idea of carrying a nuclear payload into space is nothing new. The aborted 1970 Apollo 13 moon mission was made all the more treacherous by the fact that the spaceship was carrying plutonium, a fact conveniently ignored in the myth-making 1995 film, *Apollo 13*. However, it wasn't until late 1997 that the U.S. government really got serious about irradiating the heavens.

An October 1997 launch from the Kennedy Space Center in Florida sent a probe called Cassini—with 72.3 pounds of plutonium on board—rocketing into space. According to Helen Caldicott, plutonium is "so toxic that less than one-millionth of a gram, an invisible particle, is a carcinogenic dose. One pound, if uniformly distributed, could hypothetically induce lung cancer in every person on Earth."[47]

Before Caldicott's hypothetical is deemed capricious, one might wish to consider that the Russians have a fifteen percent failure rate with nuclear payloads and the U.S. has already launched twenty-four devices carrying nuclear material into space (all with *considerably* less than 72.3 pounds) and three have met with accidents. This includes the aforementioned Apollo 13.

"Before the Challenger accident," adds journalist Karl Grossman, "NASA based the likelihood of a catastrophe at 1 in 100,000. Then came the Challenger, and now it's 1 in 74. [It] just shows how ridiculous these claims by NASA are."[48]

The Gulf War provided yet another opportunity for the United States to expand upon WWII's immoral nuclear legacy. By assigning Hitler status to Saddam Hussein and thereby assigning good war status to Operation Desert Storm, the U.S. secured the freedom to bomb at will. Despite a UN resolution of December 4, 1990 specifically prohibiting attacks on Iraq's nuclear facilities, the U.S. made no secret of its plans to target such sites. Within eight days of the first attacks on Iraq, General Colin Powell publicly proclaimed that Hussein's "two operating reactors...are both gone. They're down. They're finished." One week later, General H. Norman Schwarzkopf announced that allied forces had attacked eighteen chemical, ten biological, and three nuclear plants.[49]

"As usual," says media analyst Edward Herman, "the media paid no attention whatever to possible U.S. war crimes, such as attacks on nuclear reactors."

However, it wasn't only Iraqi atomic material polluting the environment; thanks to depleted uranium (DU) armor-piercing shells, the United States did more than its share of spreading the radioactivity. Here's how James Ridgeway described DU in the January 15, 1991 *Village Voice*:

> When fired, the uranium bursts into flame and all but liquifies, searing through steel armor like a white hot phosphorescent flare. The heat of the shell causes any diesel fuel vapors in the enemy tank to explode, and the crew inside is burned alive.

As grisly as that may sound, the effects of DU did not end with the scorched bodies of Iraqi conscripts. "The uranium-238 used to make the weapons can cause cancer and genetic defects when inhaled," says Ramsey Clark.[50]

"Depleted uranium burns on contact," adds Caldicott, "creating tiny aerosolized particles less than five microns in diameter, small enough to be inhaled." These minute particles can travel "long distances when airborne," explains Dr. Caldicott.

During the war, some 940,000 small DU shells were fired from U.S. planes and 14,000 larger shells from tanks. "Further," Caldicott states, "on two separate occasions vehicles loaded with uranium shells accidentally exploded, showering friends and foes alike with tiny respirable particles of deadly uranium."[51]

While DU irradiation has quite predictably wrought havoc on the overall ecology of Iraq and Kuwait for generations to come, it's also managed to find its way back into the U.S.—thanks to the returning Gulf War veterans.

"The widespread use of DU in the Gulf War can be directly linked to the Gulf War Syndrome," says Michio Kaku.[52]

As reported by Laura Flanders in the March 7, 1994 issue of *The Nation*, the U.S. Department of Veterans Affairs conducted a state-wide survey of Gulf War veterans in Mississippi. It was found that 67 percent of the children conceived by these veterans since the end of the war were born with severe illnesses or birth defects.

"The United States has conducted two nuclear wars," Caldicott concludes. "The first against Japan in 1945, the second in Kuwait and Iraq in 1991."

The price we all pay for the low-level radiation since the end of WWII has become an inescapable part of our everyday lives: a compromised immune system and a corresponding rise in opportunistic pathogens. As reported by Steve Eckardt in *Third World Resurgence*, Drs. Andrei Sakharov and Ernest Sternglass have studied the phenomenon of low-level radiation and its "lethal effects on the immune system." The doctors have found, for example, that "effects of the Chernobyl accidents were even apparent in small but statistically significant excess mortality in the United States in May 1986."[53] This reality only makes it more difficult to comprehend the widespread use of radiation and nuclear medicine as a method of "curing." Surely everyone can recount the experience of having a technician offer reassuring words about the safety of X-rays as she or he scurries to hide behind a nearby wall.

"I think, as a word to the wise, that everyone should reduce the amount of X-rays they get," says Michio Kaku, "...unless it's [a] life-threatening [situation]."[54]

What about the use of radiation—a proven cause of cancer—to treat cancer? What of the claims of the American Medical Association, as early as 1947, that "medically applied atomic science has already saved more lives than we lost in the explosions at Hiroshima and Nagasaki."?[55]

"The procedure has actually been shown to be useful in only a small number of cancers," writes health advocate John Robbins. "With these significant and noteworthy exceptions, the vast majority of studies show that radiation cannot cure cancer, and that it can rarely extend life for people with the disease."[56]

The technology that ended WWII has also found its way into the typical American's food supply. "The Department of Energy, responsible for disposing of our vast stockpiles of nuclear by-products," says health advisor, Gary Null, "has proposed that we expose food to radiation."[57] As a result, the Food and Drug Administration (FDA) has approved what is called "food irradiation," allowing what we eat to be exposed to radiation doses from 100,000 to 6,000,000 times that of a chest X-ray.

And if it's not in your food, it's in the pots and pans you cook with and the table you sit at and that shiny ring on your finger and, well, you get the idea.

An article in the January/February 1999 issue of *Spectrum: The Wholistic News Magazine*, details a novel method—*already in use*—of disposing of the waste created by half a century of nuclear operations: recycle the radioactive metals into consumer products like eating utensils, furniture, jewelry, pots, pans, eyeglasses, and more. This plan has been given the green light by the Department of Energy (DOE) and the metal industry is already lobbying to set standards that will enable them to use as much of the cheap atomic by-product as possible. Products containing recycled radioactive materials will be allowed to emit up to 10 milligrams of radiation per year, if the metal lobbyists get their way—with the obligatory claim, of course, that such a "small" dose is not dangerous.

"According to the Nuclear Regulatory Commission," writes *Spectrum*, "…a radiation dose of 10 millirems per year received continuously over a lifetime increases the risk of cancer by 4 in 10,000. This would translate to 92,755 additional cancer deaths in the U.S. alone."

As for the radioactive items already in the marketplace, a study done in the 1980s found that fourteen Americans who wore contaminated jewelry had already developed finger cancer, some of whom required amputation.

With the globe now anointed with an ample dose of atomic aromatherapy, one might accept the excuse that nuclear scientists simply did not know of the lethal side effects of radiation during the early post-war era. However, in late 1993, when then-Energy Secretary Hazel O'Leary released documents about secret nuclear experiments on American citizens, that alibi was no longer big enough to hide behind.

Immediately after Hirshoshima and Nagasaki, nuclear researchers set about, at any cost, to discern the effects of plutonium on the human body. "In experiments worthy of Dr. Mengele," writes Jack Bradigan Spula in *Lies of Our Times*, "these researchers chose unwitting patients who were not expected to live long anyway."[58]

Peter Montague is director of the Environmental Research Foundation. "There were two kinds of experiments," he says. "In one kind, specific small groups (African-American prisoners, mentally retarded children, and others) were induced, by money or by verbal subterfuge, to submit to irradiation of one kind or another. In all, some 800 individuals participated in these 'guinea pig' trials. In the second kind, large civilian populations were exposed to intentional releases of radioactive isotopes into the atmosphere."[59]

The corporate media response to these revelations was as to be expected. For example, *Newsweek* (December 27, 1993) had this to say about the 204 unannounced nuclear explosions and 600 experiments on humans:

> The scientists who had conducted those tests so long ago surely had rational reasons: the struggle with the Soviet Union, the fear of imminent nuclear war, the urgent need to unlock all the secrets of the atom, for purposes both military and medical.[60]

Despite media acquiescence, these vile experiments cannot genuinely be dismissed as a momentary lapse amidst a well-intentioned, post-"Good War" paranoia. The declassified documents on U.S. radiation experiments stretch three miles long.[61]

NO NUKES

I'm one of the lucky ones. The deadly legacy of the Manhattan Project hasn't directly affected me yet, at least as far as I can tell. I don't live in a Third World nation that's been bombed into oblivion in the name of making the world safe for democracy. I'm not a former welfare recipient whose checks have stopped coming because the government needed more money for those bombs. I haven't been unknowingly injected with radiation at a federal hospital.

However, as I sit in New York City writing this, I am reminded that the Indian Point nuclear reactor is only thirty-five miles from the center of Manhattan and, as Dr. Caldicott details, "A meltdown would…[trap] millions of people in a radioactive hell, unable to escape, dying within forty-eight hours of acute radiation illness. Such an event is not unlikely according to the Nuclear Regulatory Commission, because this reactor is plagued with safety problems."

We're all downwinders.

NOTES FOR CHAPTER SIX

1. Udall, p. 32
2. Stauber and Rampton, p. 33
3. Shalom, p. 78
4. Kenneth C. Davis, p. 316
5. Davis, p. 316
6. Udall, p. 367
7. Udall, p. 41
8. Udall, p. 439
9. Takaki, p. 6
10. Robert Jay Lifton and Greg Mitchell. *Hiroshima in America: Fifty Years of Denial* (New York: Grosset/Putnam, 1995), p. 56
11. William Blum, "Hiroshima: Needless Slaughter, Useful Terror," *Covert Action Quarterly*, Summer 1995, p. 23 (*Covert Action Quarterly* is a Washington, DC-based political journal.)
12. Gar Alperovitz. *The Decision to Use the Atomic Bomb and the Architecture of an American Myth* (New York: A. A. Knopf, 1995), p. 515
13. Alperovitz, p. 516-7
14. Blum, *CAQ*, pp. 23, 23n., 25
15. Takaki, p. 23
16. Blum, *CAQ*, p. 23
17. Zinn, p. 414
18. Takaki, p. 100
19. Shalom, p. 78
20. Blum, *CAQ*, p. 24
21. Zinn, pp. 413-4
22. Blum, *CAQ*, p. 25
23. Takaki, p. 7
24. Takaki, p. 7
25. Takaki, p. 7
26. Blum, *CAQ*, p. 25
27. Davis, p. 318
28. Charles L. Mee. *Meeting at Potsdam* (New York: M. Evans, 1975), p. 239
29. Terkel is quoted from an interview with Miles Harvey in *In These Times*, August 7, 1995.
30. Lifton & Mitchell, p. 25
31. Lifton & Mitchell, p. 41
32. Lifton & Mitchell, pp. 47-9, 55
33. Shalom, p. 79
34. Takaki, pp. 142-3
35. Blum, *CAQ*, p. 25

36. Shalom, p. 79

37. Zinn, p. 415

38. Adams, p. 67

39. Mark C. Carnes, ed. *Past Imperfect: History According to the Movies* (New York: Henry Holt and Company, 1995), p. 249

40. Carnes, p. 249

41. Carnes, p. 248

42. *World Almanac & Book of Facts*, p. 75

43. William Preston, Jr., "Our Friend the Atom," *LOOT*, Jan.-Feb. 1994, pp. 23-5

44. Ambrose, p. 472

45. Helen Caldicott. *Nuclear Madness: What You Can Do* (New York: W.W. Norton and Company, 1978, 1994), p. 174. (For all Caldicott references on Hanford.)

46. John Downey. "*LOOT* Interviews Carole Gallagher," *Lies of Our Times*, April 1994: pp. 14-8 (for all of Gallagher's quotes)

47. Quoted by Bruce Gagnon in the *Cassini Fact Sheet*, Florida Coalition for Peace & Justice, 1996

48. Karl Grossman. "Nukes in Space," interviewed by David Barsamian, audiocassette, *Alternative Radio*, 1996

49. Clark, p. 97

50. Clark, p. 99

51. Caldicott; International Action Center. *Metal of Dishonor, Depleted Uranium: How the Pentagon Radiates Soldiers and Civilians with DU Weapons* (New York, IAC, 1997) pp. 18-9 (for all of her quotes in this section)

52. Kaku, *Metal*, p. 111

53. Steve Eckardt. "Global Extermination: Neither Fire Nor Water This Time," *Third World Resurgence*, #51, p. 6

54. Kaku, audio-cassette

55. John Robbins. *Reclaiming Our Health: Exploding the Medical Myth and Embracing the Source of True Healing* (Tiburon, CA: HJ Kramer, 1996), p. 230

56. Robbins, pp. 229-30

57. Gary Null. *The '90s Healthy Body Book: How to Overcome the Effects of Pollution and Cleanse the Toxins from Your Body* (Deerfield Beach, FL: Health Communications, Inc., 1994), p. 65

58. Jack Bradigan Spula. "The Untold Story of Nuclear Experiments," *Lies of Our Times*, April 1994, p. 10

59. Peter Montague. "Experiments: Radiation Then, Chemicals Now," *Lies of Our Times*, April 1994, p. 12
60. Spula, *LOOT*, p. 11
61. Kaku, audio-cassette

CHAPTER SEVEN

"There are Few Archbishops in Espionage…"

"The Allied war has been sanitized and romanticized almost beyond recognition by the sentimental, the loony patriotic, the ignorant, and the bloodthirsty."

—Paul Fussell
Wartime

he greatest blurring of the distinction between good and evil exists in the late- and post-war alliances forged by the United States. While the myriad war crimes committed by all participants in WWII could be callously explained away as inherent to any such conflict (although one may get an argument from the survivors of Auschwitz, Nanking, Dresden, Hiroshima, et. al), it stretches the limits of morality and humanity to accept any excuse for the blatant U.S. collaboration with both organized crime members and unrepentant Axis war criminals in the name of—yet again—anti-communism.

The myths of WWII grow increasingly imbedded within America's impressionable psyche, thanks to scholars and Hollywood tastemakers. Perry mentions a "massive ideological mobilization of American opinion against communism and a new apprehension about national security" during the post-war era, but a lesser-known legacy is that the "Good War" has infected the entire globe. Secret decisions and cloak-and-dagger agreements made near the end of WWII have directly spawned many of the subsequent wars, border conflicts, bloody coups, and assorted military interventions since that time. As Allen Dulles, a major player in many of these cynical and misguided covert operations, once remarked, "An intelligence service is an ideal vehicle for a conspiracy."[1]

ALL IN THE FAMILY

The "enemy-of-my-enemy-is-my-friend" justification for foreign intervention became carved-in-stone policy when the U.S. government cozied up to American and Sicilian organized crime figures—in the name of fighting, well, organized crime.

"In the first three months following Pearl Harbor," writes Robert Lacey, "the United States and its allies lost more than 120 merchant ships to German U-boats in the waters off the American coast."[2] Suspicion of enemy infiltration grew and the investigative section of U.S. Naval Intelligence in the New York area, the B-3, began to collaborate with mobsters who dominated the New York City docks. Their first contact was Joseph "Socks" Lanza, but with multiple racketeering indictments, Lanza's motives began to be questioned by his cohorts. It was time to for the B-3 to aim higher. "Operation Underworld," as the Navy called it, led directly to Lucky Luciano.

Salvatore C. Luciana, a.k.a. Charles "Lucky" Luciano, was known as the first of the modern Mafia bosses. He had been in prison since 1936 and, as of May 1942, still had twenty-four years of his sentence to serve, followed by inevitable deportation orders. However, Luciano wasn't nicknamed "Lucky" for nothing—he had something the Navy wanted and all they needed was to find a like-minded soul to convince him to share. In 1942, the Navy reached out to Meyer Lansky.[3]

A mobster of legendary reputation, Lansky—once dubbed "the Mafia's Henry Kissinger" by comedian Jackie Mason—was already active in domestic anti-Nazi circles when the navy contacted him. As Lacey documents, Lansky and his henchmen would regularly break up pro-Nazi meetings in the U.S. during the mid-1930s. On one occasion, journalist Walter Winchell tipped off the underworld chieftain about a gathering that would feature none other than the leader of the German-American Bund, Fritz Kuhn, scheduled to take place in Yorkville, Manhattan's German neighborhood. Lansky recalled that night as follows:

> We got there that evening and found several hundred people dressed in their brown shirts. The stage was decorated with a swastika and pictures of Hitler…There were only about fifteen of us, but we went into action."[4]

"Lansky's volunteers threw firecrackers and started fights," says Lacey, "so that the meeting degenerated into chaos." As a result, the assembled audience did not get to hear Fritz Kuhn speak that night.[5]

With a proven anti-Nazi background and many years of lucrative collaboration with Luciano as collateral, Meyer Lansky was a natural for Operation Underworld. In no time, he had Luciano transferred to Great Meadow, "the state's unprison-looking prison" in the town of Comstock, sixty miles north of Albany. "We went up by train to Albany," Lansky recalled, "and from Albany we get a car to take us to the prison."[6]

Almost overnight, stories of lavish banquets became commonplace, although prison authorities and New York Governor Thomas Dewey denied such allegations.

Luciano put out the word on June 4, 1942, and by June 27, eight German secret agents were arrested in New York and Chicago thanks to information provided by patriots who moonlighted as murderers, loan sharks, and gamblers. In November of that same year, with Socks Lanza mediating, a threatened longshoreman's strike was averted—much to the navy's delight.

It wasn't long before the U.S. government would call on its favorite professional criminals for help in the actual fighting of

WWII. As the Allies took control of North Africa and began to contemplate an assault on Sicily, military planners realized that they were too unfamiliar with the coastline of the Italian island to undertake such a venture. In a flash, Lansky recruited an illegal gambling cohort, Joe Adonis, to dig up some Sicilians in New York City. Soon, these *padrones*, as they were called, were meeting at the headquarters for navy intelligence at 90 Church Street to peruse a giant map of their homeland. As Lacey documents, the results are, as they say, history:

> In the small hours of July 10, 1943, Lieutenant Paul Alfieri landed on Licata Beach and made contact with local Sicilians who told him the secret location of Italian Naval Command, hidden in a nearby holiday vista. Inside, Alfieri discovered 'the entire disposition of the Italian and German Naval forces in the Mediterranean—together with mine-fields located in the Mediterranean area—together with overlays of these minefields, prepared by the Germans, showing the safe-conduct routes through the mines.'[7]

Once the Allies had landed in Sicily and met with Luciano's contacts, they were aided on the ground throughout the entire venture. This was especially true for General George S. Patton, the commander of the Seventh Army.

"Patton was a general of extraordinary martial dexterity, but the sixty thousand troops and countless booby traps in his path should have given him at least a few problems," says Vankin. "His way has been cleared by Sicily's Mafia boss Calogero Vizzini, at the request of Luciano."[8]

While Lansky's biographer, Robert Lacey, downplays such stories, he does mention "dark tales of planes dropping flags and handkerchiefs bearing the letter *L* behind enemy lines—signals, supposedly, from Luciano to local mafia chieftains."[9]

Regardless of the methods used to recruit unabashed murderers into a battle against unabashed mass murderers, anti-communism was again the overriding motivation. Since much of Italy's anti-fascist resistance was made up of leftists and communists, the Mafia was a willing partner in smashing such sentiment. As Sicily was secured by the Allies, "the occupying American Army appointed Mafia bosses—including Vizzini—[as] mayors of many Sicilian townships," says Vankin. "Gangsters became an American-backed quasi-police force." When Vizzini killed the police chief in Villaba, the town where he was appointed mayor, he was not prosecuted.

"In American-occupation headquarters, one of the best employees was Vito Genovese, who eventually inherited Luciano's New York operation," adds Vankin.

Upon the war's end, Luciano was granted executive clemency by New York governor Thomas Dewey and was released (albeit for deportation) on January 4, 1946. What the mob boss did with his newfound freedom is yet another of the war's vile repercussions.

"From abroad," says Vankin, "Luciano...founded what might as well be called Heroin, Inc., an illegal multinational corporation." The price to be paid would be incalculable. After WWII, there were roughly 20,000 heroin addicts in the U.S. down from 200,000 twenty years earlier. By 1952, the number of addicts had tripled to 60,000. In 1965, it was 150,000. By 1990, estimates ranged from 533,000 to 1.1. million.[10]

Meyer Lansky kept his fingers in the foreign policy pie when, in an ironic turn, Zionists approached fellow Jew Lansky in 1948, for help arming Israel. He used his B-3 contacts to track down a Pittsburgh dealer who was supplying Arabs with weapons. These arms conveniently "fell overboard," and Lansky had them diverted to the new Jewish state so they could wage war on their neighbors—some of whom were battling Israel with tactics taught by another U.S. government soulmate, former SS legend Otto Skorzeny.

All of this was subsidized by American taxpayers in the name of "good."

The growth and influence of organized crime, the scourge of rampant drug abuse, and a half-century of deadly Middle East conflicts are not the only miseries hatched by U.S. intelligence agencies with a little help from the Mafia. In the nation that gave birth to La Cosa Nostra, the consequences of post-war activities are still being felt.

Making no secret of their belief that WWII was essentially a brief hiatus in the endless battle to stem the tide of godless communism, U.S. post-war policy planners instituted the Marshall Plan, under which more than $12 billion in loans and grants were provided to Europe—funds designated for return to American corporations. In 1949, for example, these funds were used to purchase a third of U.S. exports to Europe.[11]

Public relations pieties and Marshall's eventual Nobel Peace Prize aside, the ultimate goal of this program was to avoid the type of economic collapse that could possibly enhance the position of leftist and/or communist movements in post-war Europe. Towards this end, the Marshall Plan was designed to rebuild Western Europe's state-capitalist economies. One such state-capitalist economy was that of Italy, and here's where the brand new CIA got its feet wet.

"The CIA was created by the National Security Act of 1947," writes Mark Zepezauer. "The ink was barely dry on it before an army of spooks began marching through the law's major loophole: the CIA could 'perform such other functions and duties...as the National Security Council [NSC] may from time to time direct'.... One of the the first duties the NSC deemed necessary was the subversion of Italian democracy...in the name of democracy, of course."[12]

When the war-weary Italian people went to the polls in 1946, the Italian Communist Party and the Socialist Party combined to gain more votes and more seats in the Constituent Assembly election than the U.S.-favored Christian Democrats. This was not surprising, considering that a worker- and peasant-based movement fought off six German divisions during the liberation of northern

Italy—with the invaluable aid of the Communist party. As a 1948 election loomed on the horizon, however, the United States realized that certain perceptions of reality needed to be seriously altered.

"It was at this point that the U.S. began to train its big economic and political guns upon the Italian people," William Blum explains in *Killing Hope*. "All the good ol' Yankee know-how, all the Madison Avenue savvy in the art of swaying public opinion, all the Hollywood razzmatazz would be brought to bear on the 'target market'."

Downplaying the quite impressive anti-fascist credentials of the communists and the potentially embarrassing record of collaboration with Mussolini displayed by the Christian Democrats, the U.S. cleverly framed the battle around, what Blum calls "the question of 'democracy' vs. 'communism' (the idea of 'capitalism' remaining discretely to one side.)," and the most powerful election issue was that of U.S. aid.[13]

The influential American media obediently did its part with the January 21, 1947 *New York Times* proclaiming that, "Some observers here feel that a further Leftward swing in Italy would retard aid." By March 22, 1948, *Time* magazine was labeling a potential leftist victory in Italy to be nothing short of "the brink of catastrophe." As the election neared, the CIA pulled out all the stops.

Blum has documented some of the steps taken in this "awesome mobilization of resources." A few representative examples should offer a idea of the propaganda's scope and depth:

- A letter-writing campaign from Italian-Americans to their friends and families in Italy was guided by "sample letters" provided by the U.S., that included such passages as: "A communist victory would ruin Italy. The United States would withdraw aid and a world war would probably result."
- Short-wave broadcasts to Italy warned that "under a communist dictatorship in Italy," many of the "nation's indus-

trial plants would be dismantled and shipped to Russia and millions of Italy's workers would be deported to Russia for forced labor."

- The stars of Hollywood, like Gary Cooper and Frank Sinatra, were called upon to make Voice of America radio broadcasts and/or engage in fundraisers for causes like "the orphans of Italian pilots who died in the war."
- As for more direct aid, the CIA admitted to giving $1 million to Italian "center parties," although Blum says the figure could be as high as $10 million.[14]

In case all the funny stuff failed, the CIA also took the precaution of organizing Operation Gladio, a secret paramilitary group in Italy, "with hidden stockpiles of weapons and explosives dotting the map," says Zepezauer. While the rationale for such intervention was the always-handy "threat of Soviet invasion," Zepezauer reveals the actual purpose of Operation Gladio, i.e. its "15,000 troops were trained to overthrow the Italian government should it stray from the straight and narrow."[15]

They needn't have bothered because, after the circus left town, the Christian Democrats stood as the clear winner with 48 percent of the vote.[16] The future course of Italy had effectively been charted—not by a fair and open democratic election, but instead via the subversion of organized criminal syndicates like the Mafia and the CIA.

THE CLASS OF '45

Even before the CIA was the CIA, it was acting an awful lot like the CIA. According to Christopher Simpson, the journalist who has perhaps done more work than any other in the area of U.S. recruitment of ex-Nazis, an August 16, 1983 Justice Department report "acknowledged that a U.S. intelligence agency known as the Army Counterintelligence Corps (CIC) had recruited Schutzstaffel (SS) and Gestapo officer Klaus Barbie for espionage work in early 1947; that the CIC had hidden him from French war crimes investigators; and that it had then spirited him out of Europe through a clandestine 'ratline'—escape route—run by a priest who was himself a fugitive from war crimes charges."[17]

The report went on to state that the CIC agents had no idea at the time what Barbie had done during the war (apparently, having to hide him from French war crimes investigators didn't set off any alarms), and that Barbie was the only such war criminal that the U.S. had protected.

We'll come back to the Butcher of Lyon later; for now, let's examine the specious claim that he was the only former Nazi welcomed into the American espionage fold.

"The pattern was set," writes Noam Chomsky, "in the first area liberated by U.S. forces, North Africa, where in 1942 the U.S. placed in power Admiral Jean Darlan, a leading Nazi collaborator who was the author of the Vichy regime's anti-Semitic laws." Even WWII's official historian, Stephen Ambrose, has admitted:

> The result was that in its first major foreign-policy venture in World War II, the United States gave its support to a man who stood for everything Roosevelt and Churchill had spoken out against in the Atlantic Charter. As much as Goering or Goebbels, Darlan was the antithesis of the principles the Allies said they were struggling to establish.[18]

Darlan was merely the first step in a premeditated program of collaboration with notorious war criminals.

"I am a general and chief of the intelligence department of the High Command of the German Army. I have information of the highest importance for your Supreme Commander and the American government, and I must be taken immediately to your senior commander."[19]

It was with these words that General Reinhard Gehlen, Hitler's notorious eastern front espionage chief, began his relationship with the Office of Strategic Services (OSS) and the budding U.S. intelligence community. As the OSS was transformed into the Central Intelligence Agency (CIA), yet another of many dark alliances emerged.

After surrendering on May 22, 1945, Gehlen, or "Reinhard the Fox," was eventually interviewed by OSS founders "Wild" Bill Donovon and Allen Dulles after flying to Washington in the uniform of a U.S. general. According to his biographer, Leonard Mosley, Dulles recommended that the Nazi superspy be given a budget of $3,500,000 and "set up in business as the supplier of Russian and east European intelligence."[20] But the shrewd Gehlen had some conditions:

1. His organization would not be regarded as part of the American intelligence services but as an autonomous apparatus under his exclusive management. Liaison with American intelligence would be maintained by a U.S. officer whose selection Gehlen would approve.

2. The Gehlen Organization would be used solely to procure intelligence on the Soviet Union and the satellite countries of the communist bloc.

3. Upon the establishment of a German government, the organization would be transferred to it and all previous agreements and arrangements cancelled, subject to discussions between the new sovereign authority and the United States.

4. Nothing detrimental or contrary to German interests must be required or expected from the organization, nor must it be called upon for security activities against Germans in West Germany.

Considering that Gehlen was essentially a prisoner of war who could have been brought up on war crimes, these demands were remarkable. Even more remarkable, at first blush, is the fact that the U.S. complied. However, when viewed through the prism of the rapidly escalating Cold War, a Nazi-CIA alliance becomes rather predictable.

With German defeat imminent, Gehlen instructed several members of his staff to begin microfilming intelligence on the USSR beginning in March 1945. After secretly burying this material throughout the Austrian Alps, Gehlen and his men sought a deal.

Upon his surrender, Gehlen was taken to Fort Hunt, Virginia, where he convinced his U.S. counterparts that the Soviets were planning a westward expansion.[21] Before the end of 1945, Gehlen and most of his high command were freed from POW camps and ready to supply what rabid American cold warriors were dying to hear.

By way of torture, interrogation, and mass starvation of the four million-plus Soviet POWs at his disposal, Gehlen procured the information that would save him and some of his Third Reich cohorts from the gallows. Among these men was SS *Obersturmführer* Hans Sommer, widely known for setting fire to seven Paris synagogues in October 1941.[22] Gehlen, and his staff eventually became known as "the Gehlen Org," which was funded by the United States until a new German government came to power. For nearly a full decade, the Gehlen Org was essentially the CIA's singular source for Eastern European intelligence.[23] The fruits of this relationship manifested themselves in a deadly Cold War and, true to his job experiences in the war-torn Soviet Union, Reinhard the Fox did whatever it took to stay in business.

"Gehlen had to make his money by creating a threat that we were afraid of, so we would give him more money to tell us about it," explains Victor Marchetti, formerly the CIA's chief analyst of Soviet strategic war plans and capabilities.[24]

When Allen Dulles became CIA Director in 1953, (brother John was already Eisenhower's Secretary of State by that time), his response to the claim that Gehlen, a known Nazi war criminal, was purposely intensifying the Cold War and influencing American public opinion was:

I don't know if he's a rascal. There are few archbishops in

espionage…Besides, one needn't ask him to one's club.[25]

Playing Rambo to Reinhard Gehlen's James Bond was Otto "Scarface" Skorzeny, commonly referred to by the German press as "Hitler's favorite commando."

"At six feet four inches and 220 pounds," Simpson writes, "with appropriately arrogant 'Aryan' features and a five-inch dueling scar down his left cheek, Skorzeny had transformed himself during the war from an unknown SS truck driver into a walking symbol of Nazi strength and cunning."[26] This reputation was cemented thanks to his daring rescue of Benito Mussolini when the dictator's enemies in Italy placed him under house arrest in 1943.

Mussolini was initially imprisoned on the island of Ponza, some thirty-five miles off the coast of Italy. Using contacts cultivated by German agents well-established within the Italian hierarchy, Skorzeny learned of Il Duce's whereabouts and of his subsequent transfer to the Gran Sasso skiing area of Apennine Mountains. The hulking *Sturmbannführer* then proceeded to execute a stunning rescue against impossible odds, thus ingratiating himself with his Führer.[27]

"Hitler loved him," says Simpson. Dulles took a liking to him, too.

Like Gehlen, Skorzeny also surrendered himself to the U.S. in the last hours of the Third Reich—after which he was promptly acquitted of war crimes and managed to "escape" from an internment camp, leaving behind a note that proclaimed that he had "only done my duty to my Fatherland."

In the ensuing years, Scarface Skorzeny worked his mayhem while on the CIA payroll. It was in Egypt, in the late 40s and early 50s, that the Nazi killer left his mark on the international theater. At the special request of Reinhard Gehlen, the CIA sent Skorzeny to replace King Farouk with an Egyptian general named Mohammed Naguib. Scarface felt at home in the Middle East where he saw a chance to renew his anti-Semitic, fascist propensities. He threw his support behind rising star Gamal Abdel Nasser and used CIA money to import over 100 former SS cronies to aid in his machinations.

Among these recruits were Adolf Eichmann's chief aide, Alois Brunner, a man said to be responsible for 128,500 murders[28]; Hermann Lauterbacher, former deputy leader of the Hitler Youth; and Franz Buensch, a propagandist who worked for Goebbels and authored the pornographic book, *The Sexual Habits of Jews*.[29]

In his spare time, Skorzeny began training the earliest Palestinian freedom fighters. Scarface's protegés ended up doing battle against an enemy well-armed by American taxpayers via underworld kingpin Meyer Lansky.

Other salaried U.S. recruits from the pool of available murderers included:[30]

- The aforementioned Brunner (a.k.a. "Georg Fischer"), sentenced to death (in abstensia) by the French government for crimes against humanity. In 1953, after he was put to work with Scarface Skorzeny, Brunner/Fischer was considered by many to be "the most depraved Nazi killer still at large." He was known for his lack of compassion for Jewish children, labeling them "future terrorists" who must be murdered.

- SS officer Baron Otto von Bolschwing, a senior aide to the notorious Adolf Eichmann, who assisted in drawing up the SS's "first comprehensive program for the systematic robbery of Europe's Jews." Under orders from von Bolschwing, some of the many Jewish victims in a 1941 Bucharest pogrom were butchered in a meat packing plant, hung on hooks, and literally branded as "kosher meat," while others—including a five-year-old girl—were skinned alive and left hanging by their feet like slaughtered livestock. Von Bolschwing himself stated that in 1945, "he volunteered his services to the Army CIC, which used him for interrogation and recruitment of other former Nazi intelligence officers"—an offer the U.S. readily accepted.

- SS Obersturmführer Robert Verbelen, who had once been "sentenced to death in abstentia for war crimes, including the torture of two U.S. Air Force pilots." After the war, he served in Vienna as a contract spy for the U.S. Army, which was completely aware of his background.

- Dr. Kurt Blome, "who admitted in 1945 that he had been a leader of Nazi biological warfare research, a program known to have included experimentation on prisoners in concentration camps." In 1947, he was acquitted of crimes against humanity and then hired by the U.S. Army Chemical Corps "to conduct a new round of biological weapons research."

- Blome's colleague, Dr. Arthur Rudolph, "who was accused in sworn testimony at Nuremberg of committing atrocities at the Nazis' underground rocket works near Nordhausen but was later given U.S. citizenship and a major role in the U.S. missile program."

Finally, there was General Walter Dornberger, who was never indicted or tried for war crimes, but was brought over to this country by the U.S. Air Force in 1947 for his expertise in rocketry and missile technology.

What the air force and Corporate America chose to ignore is the fact that much of Dornberger's research at the underground Nazi factory near Nordhausen was carried out with help of slave labor from the nearby Dora concentration camp. At least 20,000 prisoners were killed in the course of Dornberger's project.[31]

While it may be pointed out that Dornberger did not directly control the slaves used to do his work, he did set the schedule that eventually worked them to death. Even after food ran out for the slave laborers in early 1945, Dornberger, who had visited the Nordhausen factory on many occasions and was familiar with the goings-on there, never slowed down his work orders.[32]

Despite all this, once he was safely in Cold War-crazed America, the valuable Herr Dornberger rose to the level of senior vice-president in the Bell Aerosystems Division of Textron Corporation and died a well-respected anti-communist in 1980.

Reinhard the Fox, Scarface Skorzeny, and the other members of the Rogues Gallery featured above were not the only Nazis Dulles would proudly claim to be "on our side" by the end of the war.

The CROWCRASS (the central registry for tracing war crimes suspects) project, which began in May 1945, had processed, in its first three years, 85,000 wanted reports, transmitted 130,000 detention reports, and published 40 book-length registries of persons being sought. This extensive research served to not only track down those eventually put on trial, but also those who could help the U.S.—and this included more than military men. Between 1945 and 1955, 765 scientists, engineers, and technicians were brought to America. Roughly 80 percent were former Nazi party members or SS men.

The Soviets, for their part, also recruited from the ranks of ex-Nazis. One prime example was SS General Hans Rattenhuber, formerly the commander of Hitler's personal SS guard, who became a senior East German political police official in East Berlin.

While any Soviet interaction with Hitler's former minions was welcome grist for America's media/propaganda mill, U.S. involvement with war criminals remained, for the most part, under wraps.

To help keep the public oblivious, in 1948, the National Committee for a Free Europe (NCFE) was formed to aid exiles from Soviet-occupied Eastern Europe. In reality, it was "launched to serve as a thinly veiled 'private-sector' cover through which clandestine U.S. funds" could be passed to anti-communist governments-in-exile. The seed money of two million dollars was drawn from a pool of captured German assets.

The NCFE board of directors included J. Peter Grace of W.R. Grace and Company and the National City Bank; H.J. Heinz of the Mellon Bank and Heinz tomato ketchup fame; Henry Ford II; and film directors Darryl Zanuck and Cecil B. De Mille. Also involved was James B. Carey of the CIO, who bluntly remarked, "In the last war we joined with the Communists to fight the Fascists. In another war we will join the Fascists to defeat the Communists."

Even though the board also included Henry Luce (publisher of Time-Life) and DeWitt Wallace (publisher of *Reader's Digest*), the sources of financing for the NCFE were never mentioned in the press. "The practical effect of this arrangement was a creation of a powerful lobby inside American media that tended to suppress critical news concerning the CIA's propaganda projects," explains Simpson.[33]

How does the CIA explain their post-WWII activities—some of which involved working side-by-side with mass murderers in order to raise the stakes in an already pernicious Cold War?

"We are not Boy Scouts," agency director Richard Helms reminded us in the late 1960s.[34]

THE BUTCHER SETS UP SHOP

Perhaps the best-known Nazi refugee to enjoy the hospitality of American intelligence agents was the wartime chief of Gestapo in Lyon, France, Klaus Barbie. During WWII, Barbie was responsible for the deportation of Jews to death camps and the torture and murder of resistance fighters. Despite claims to the contrary, it stretches the limits of credulity to accept that U.S. intelligence was not aware of his past.

After the war, as noted at the beginning of this chapter, the notorious Butcher of Lyon was supplied by the CIC with a new identity ("Klaus Altmann") and set up in South America. In Bolivia, Barbie/Altmann set up a fascist network that served as a direct link between Nazi Germany and Central America.

A major part of that link was the establishment of the U.S. Army's School of the Americas (originally located in the Panama Canal zone and now operating at Fort Benning in Georgia). This school, designed to train Latin American military men in the not-so-gentle art of persuasion, was created in 1951. Within three years, thirteen of the twenty Latin American countries were ruled by military dictatorships.

John Loftus investigated Nazi war criminals for the U.S. Justice Department. "In the year 2025," he later wrote in the July 1985 *Boston Review*, "when the Central American death squad documents are released in the National Archives to take their place alongside the records of Nazi genocide, I am going to take my grandchildren for a visit." Loftus expressed his belief that, from such a visit, the children would learn that "those who do not know the mistakes of history are condemned to repeat them."

Perhaps the first mistake is trusting the propaganda put forth by a monopoly capitalist hierarchy.

WINNERS AND LOSERS

Unrepentant cold warriors and anti-communists can dismiss these illicit relationships with the Mafia and the SS as overzealousness in the midst of a noble mission. The ends justify the means. To gain a perspective on the ultimate consequences of such immoral alliances and the lethal Cold War deception they brought about, one should consult the democratically-elected Third World leaders, like Patrice Lumumba, Jacobo Arbenz, and Salvador Allende, who lost their nations and their lives in the madness of a conflict between superpowers. Or maybe it might be best to ask your average Afghani what he or she thinks of the deliberate exacerbation of U.S.-Soviet hostilities by men who once stood proudly alongside Adolf Hitler. How about an East Timorese or a Czech or maybe an Indonesian opposition leader? What would they say about Allen Dulles, Meyer Lansky, and Otto Skorzeny?

In 1951, Guatemalan president Juan José Arévalo (whose term gave that country a ten-year respite from military rule during which he provoked U.S. ire by modeling his government "in many ways after the Roosevelt New Deal") stepped down to be replaced by his ill-fated successor and kindred spirit, the aforementioned Arbenz. A mere three years later, a CIA-sponsored coup—to prevent the threat of a Soviet invasion, of course—stole Guatemala from its people and set the Central American nation spiraling downward into a cycle of repression, poverty, and political mass murder.

This to what Arévalo had to say about the aftermath of the war known as "good":

The arms of the Third Reich were broken and conquered...but in the ideological dialogue...Roosevelt lost the war. The real winner was Hitler.[35]

NOTES FOR CHAPTER SEVEN

1. Vankin, p. 178
2. Robert Lacey. *Little Man: Meyer Lansky and the Gangster Life* (Boston: Little, Brown and Company, 1991) p. 114.
3. Lacey, p. 5
4. Lacey, p. 113
5. While the image of 15 mobsters outwitting several hundred Nazis may seem comical at the very worst, the larger question is: where does this fit into a good war? How does U.S. collaboration with career criminals jibe with the myths surrounding WWII?
6. Lacey, p. 118
7. Lacey, p. 125
8. Vankin, p. 160
Lacey, pp. 124-5
10. Vankin, p. 159, for quote about Genovese and heroin statistics up to 1965. For 1990, heroin addiction estimates were taken from U.S. government sources (www.whitehousedrugpolicy.gov).
11. Noam Chomsky, *What Uncle Sam Really Wants* (Berkeley: Odonian Press, 1992), p. 15
12. Mark Zepezauer. *The CIA's Greatest Hits* (Tucson: Odonian Press, 1994), p. 8
13. Blum, p. 28
14. Blum, p. 32 (for all examples)
15. Zepezauer, p. 8
16. Blum, p. 34
17. Christopher Simpson. *Blowback: America's Recruitment of Nazis and its Effect on the Cold War* (New York: Weidenfeld & Nicolson, 1988), viii. The large majority of Nazi-recruiting material referred to in this chapter is from Simpson. Also, see my article, "Acthung, Baby: The Nazi-CIA Connection," Hawk, October 1992, pp. 56-60
18. Chomsky, *Turning the Tide: U.S. Intervention in Central America and the Struggle for Peace* (Boston: South End Press, 1985) p. 195 (for Darlan and Ambrose references)
19. *Hawk*, p. 58
20. *Hawk*, p. 58 (for Dulles quote and Gehlen's conditions)
21. Zepezauer, p. 6
22. Simpson, p. 45
23. Zepezauer, p. 7

24. Simpson, p. 65
25. Simpson, p. 260
26. Simpson, p. 250
27. Richard B. Lyttle. *Il Duce: The Rise and Fall of Benito Mussolini* (New York: Antheum, 1987), p. 171
28. Vankin, p. 177
29. Simpson, p. 251
30. Simpson, pp. xiii, 248, 254-5 (for details all "recruits")
31. Simpson, p. 28
32. Simpson, p. 29
33. Simpson, p. 127 (for all NCFE information)
34. Vankin, p. 172
35. Blasier, Cole. *The Hovering Giant* (Pittsburgh: University of Pittsburgh Press, 1976), p. 57ff.

CHAPTER EIGHT

"The Adjective and the Noun Don't Match..."

"As things are now going, the peace we will make, the peace we seem to be making, will be a peace of oil, a peace of gold, a peace of shipping, a peace, in brief...without moral purpose or human interest...."

—Archibald MacLeish,
Poet and
Assistant Secretary of State
during WWII

he "Good War" had been won. Now what? Well, besides actively recruiting Nazis and bringing humanity to the brink of nuclear Armageddon, the winners did have a plan. An internal document, written in 1948 by George Kennan, head of the State Department planning staff in the early post-war period, highlights the philosophy behind the U.S. strategy:

> ...We have about 50% of the world's wealth, but only 6.3% of its population.... In this situation, we cannot fail to be the object of envy and resentment. Our real task in the coming period is to devise a pattern of relationships which will permit us to maintain this position of disparity without positive detriment to our national security. To do so, we will have to dispense with all sentimentality and day-dreaming; and our attention will have to be concentrated everywhere on our immediate national objectives. We need not deceive ourselves that we can afford today the luxury of altruism and world-benefaction.... We should cease to talk about vague and—for the Far East—unreal objectives as human rights, the raising of living standards, and

democratization. The day is not far off when we are going to have to deal in straight power concepts. The less we are then hampered by idealistic slogans, the better.[1]

Thus the post-war era and the age of Cold War propaganda commenced—driven by corporate globalism and virulent anti-communism. The few years spent fighting fascism during WWII were essentially nothing more than a subtle diversion from a larger war to control resources and smash any ideology deemed incompatible with that control. When the dust had cleared, fascism had survived the saturation bombings, the genocide, and the atomic weapons to rise again in a new, more insidious form. The development of the highly unaccountable multinational corporation is one of the saddest legacies of WWII.

Accordingly, Australian scholar Alex Carey has noted the three developments of great political importance that characterize the twentieth century: "...the growth of democracy, the growth of corporate power, and the growth of corporate propaganda as a means of protecting corporate power against democracy."[2] Simply, democratic institutions can hinder the pursuit of capital, so it becomes necessary to create the false arguments discussed earlier. This helps explain how the Department of War was reborn as the Defense Department after WWII.

This also helps explain Perry's banal lessons about democracy prevailing and "democratic institutions and values" spreading "throughout the globe."

FROM GOOD WAR TO COLD WAR

What had actually spread throughout the globe had very little in common with democracy, but we must not forget that those in power were unable to enjoy the luxury of altruism. "The final answer might be an unpleasant one," Kennan explained, "but...we should not hesitate before police repression by the local government. This is not shameful since the Communists are essentially traitors.... It is better to have a strong regime in power than a liberal government if it is indulgent and relaxed and penetrated by Communists."[3]

While an exhaustive survey of the after-effects of this policy would require another volume, it is instructive to explore some samples, other than those discussed earlier, of how the "Good War" legacy begat the crimes and interventions of the Cold War—without any daydreaming about unreal objectives like human rights, of course.

Before WWII, Greece was a under right-wing monarchy and dictatorship, but the German occupation gave birth to a civil war as the National Liberation Front (EAM), an extremely popular left-wing group, and the People's Liberation Army, the guerrilla resistance wing of EAM, gained the support of the masses and were largely responsible for Greece being relatively Nazi-free by the time the British army arrived in late 1944. Viewing the EAM's early support by the Greek Communist Party and its tendency towards unrealistic slogans like education for the illiterate and welcoming women as soldiers as a precursor of what post-war Greece may be like, a British army of intervention promptly stepped in to restore the right-wing dictatorship.

In response to the jailing and repression of regime opponents and trade union leaders, a left-wing guerrilla movement sprang forth.[4] By the fall of 1946, this friction led to civil war. Great Britain, no longer able to extend itself globally, was unable to handle the rebellion and called on the U.S. for help.

"Thus it was," remarks William Blum, "that the historic task of preserving all that is decent and good in Western Civilization passed into the hands of the United States."[5]

Operating without idealistic daydreams, the U.S enthusiastically took on the task of ferreting out the communist traitors Kennan warned of (despite the fact that the Greek rebels were not receiving any aid from the Soviet Union) by setting the standard for its Cold War interventions: it sent military advisors and weapons to Greece.

"In the last five months of 1947," says Howard Zinn, "74,000 tons of military equipment were sent by the United States to the right-wing government in Athens, including artillery, dive bombers, and stocks of napalm. Two hundred and fifty army officers, headed by General James Van Fleet, advised the Greek army in the field."[6]

Foreshadowing the tenor of future U.S. entanglements, Van Fleet advised the Greek authorities to forcibly remove Greek citizens from their homes in an effort to isolate the guerrillas and drain their popular support. For the record, this episode is described by Perry as a first step in the application of the Truman Doctrine, in which the U.S. mandate was to "support free peoples who are resisting attempted subjugation by armed minorities or outside pressures."

By 1949, the civil war was over. With the leftist rebels defeated and "outside pressures" removed, Greece was free to not only maintain its high levels of poverty and illiteracy in peace, but it could now do so with the help of investment capital from Esso, Dow Chemical, and Chrysler.

Two decades later, within the context of a slightly warmer Cold War, the U.S. had to forego altruism and intervene yet again in the domestic affairs of Greece. When liberal prime minister George Papandreou was elected in 1964, it did not sit well in Washington. Things went from bad to worse when Greece further annoyed its superpower benefactor by squabbling with Turkey over Cyprus, and then objecting to U.S. plans to partition the island. Lyndon Johnson summoned the Greek ambassador for a brief lesson from the president on straight power concepts:

Fuck your parliament and your constitution. America is an elephant, Cyprus is a flea. If these two fleas continue itching the elephant, they may just get whacked by the elephant's trunk, whacked good…. We pay a lot of good American dollars to the Greeks, Mr. Ambassador. If your Prime Minister gives me a talk about democracy, parliament, and constitutions, he, his parliament, and his constitution may not last very long."[7]

Within a year, the Greek Royal Court was able to unseat Papandreou. It was later revealed that CIA Chief-in-Station in Athens, John Maury, had helped King Constantine in 1965 in the toppling of the Papandreou government.[8]

As new elections became inevitable, however, the CIA threw its considerable weight behind Colonel George Papadopoulos who had been on the Agency payroll for 15 years. Before that, he served as a captain in Nazi Security Battalions during the German occupation of Greece. The elephant most certainly did whack the flea in early 1967 when Papadopoulos seized control in a coup. Parliamentary democracy was abolished, while torture, oppression, and political murder became standard policy.

One year after the coup, the Papadopoulos military junta dutifully contributed $549,000 to the Nixon-Agnew election campaign. When the U.S. Senate called for an investigation to discern whether this money was originally funneled to the junta by the CIA, the investigation was cancelled—at the direct request of Henry Kissinger.[9]

While Greece felt the sting of a U.S. policy unhampered by idealistic slogans almost immediately after the war's end, a neighboring country had to wait a lot longer for the Truman Doctrine to take effect. It first had to survive yet another WWII-provoked civil war and over forty years of simmering rivalries.

When the Kingdom of Yugoslavia entered into an accord with fascist Germany in April 1941, it was Serb patriots in Belgrade, interestingly, who revolted.

"This led to Nazi bombing of Belgrade, a German invasion, creation of an independent fascist state in Croatia (including Bosnia-Herzegovina), and attachment of much of the Serbian province of Kosovo to Albania, than a puppet of Mussolini's Italy," explains Diana Johnstone, European editor of *In These Times* from 1979 to 1990.[10]

While many of these names should sound familiar, what is usually left out of the contemporary accounts presented by the corporate media is the smooth cooperation between the Nazis and today's good guys: the Croats and the Muslims. While the Croatians—known as Ustashe—instituted a policy of genocide against Serbs, Jews, and Gypsies, the Muslims of Bosnia and Albania made for extremely willing SS recruits.

In Serbia, German occupiers announced that for each German killed by the resistance, one hundred Serbian hostages would be executed. The threat was carried out.[11]

Despite such terror tactics, resistance did exist. The royalist Serbian group known as Chetniks, led by Draza Mihailovic, "adopted a policy of holding off attacks on the Germans in expectation of an Allied invasion," but the Partisans, led by Croatian Communist Marshal Josip Broz Tito, chose instead to fight. Tito's group "made considerable gains in the predominantly Serb border regions of Croatia and Bosnia and won support from Churchill for its effectiveness."[12]

"From scattered bands of guerrillas, [Tito's group] grew into the largest partisan movement in Europe, more than a million strong," writes Sara Flounders in *Bosnia Tragedy*. "Forty-three German divisions could not destroy the movement."

In the ensuing civil war between Chetniks and Partisans, Serb was pitted against Serb, and Tito's charges emerged victorious. "Mihailovic was executed," Johnstone states, "and school children in post-war Yugoslavia learned more about the 'fascist' nature of his Serbian nationalist Chetniks than they did about Albanian and Bosnian Muslims who had volunteered for the SS, or even about the killing of Serbs in the Jasenovac death camp run by Ustashe in Western Bosnia."[13]

Yugoslavia under Tito was able, for the most part, to remain independent of both the Soviet and American spheres of influence. However, when the U.S.S.R. began to crumble, Western capitalists moved quickly to swallow up this resource-rich area. On November 5, 1990, a year before the disintegration of the Socialist Federal Republic of Yugoslavia, the U.S. made its first move when Congress passed the 1991 Foreign Operations Appropriations Law

101-513.

"This bill was a signed death warrant," says Flounders. "One provision in particular was so lethal that even a CIA report described three weeks later in the Nov. 27, 1990, *New York Times,* predicted it would lead to a bloody civil war."[14]

The provision in question cut off all aid, trade, credits, and loans from the U.S. to Yugoslavia within six months while simultaneously ordering elections in each of the six republics that make up Yugoslavia. These elections would, of course, be subject to U.S. State Department approval.

Finally, in classic Cold War style, the law contained one final proviso: only those forces defined as "democratic forces" by the State Department would receive funding. Six months later, in tune with the law's deadline, Croatian separatists began violent demonstrations and attacked a military base. When the Yugoslav government ordered the army to intervene, civil war began. The Croatian Ustashe were back, but this time it was the Serbs who were being portrayed as fascists—thanks to the magic of propaganda.

No greater symbol of Serbian fascism existed than that of a photograph of "an emaciated man, Fikret Alic, in a group of Muslims under the blazing sun, bare-chested, behind a barbed-wire fence" in the Trnopolje refugee and transit camp, which ran in publications across the globe. In England, for example, the *Daily Mail* ran the photo under a banner of "The Proof," while the *Daily Mirror* opted for "Belsen '92."[15] In a flash, world opinion turned against the Serbs and comparisons to the Nazis were in vogue.

However, the photo was not what it seemed, says journalist Thomas Deichman. "The fact is that Alic and the other men in the famous picture were not encircled by a barbed-wire fence," he writes in the Fall 1998 *Covert Action Quarterly*. "There was no barbed-wire fence surrounding the Trnopolje refugee and transit camp. The barbed-wire was only around a small compound next to the camp, which had been erected before the war to protect agricultural products and machinery from thieves, and which the journalists had entered." As a result, the famous picture was actually taken from inside the compound as the photographer snapped at people standing outside the fence.

Following the well-worn script of WWII reconstruction, the U.S. sent military instructors to aid the Croatian Army "to woo its offices away from old, Communist habits and instill the values of a democratic army." The idea, Ed Soyster, a retired lieutenant general and former head of the Defense Intelligence Agency explained in the August 1, 1995 *New York Times*, was to run courses in "the role of the army in a democratic society." The devastating results of this strategy were manifested in a decade of war in the Balkans.

As is usually the case with war propaganda, the truth came out too late to help the victims of the lie. The U.S., Germany, and other Western powers were locked in a battle for influence and control in this resource-rich region and the Serbs, while they were certainly not innocent bystanders, were clearly not the only aggressors.

This characterization of Serbs as war criminals helped make the 1999 NATO bombing of Yugoslavia possible. The Western corporate media dutifully ignored pertinent details like the specifics of the Rambouillet agreement that Yugoslov President Slobodan Milosevic (the latest Hitler) refused to sign, and the existence of the Stari Trg mining complex—loaded with at least $5 billion worth of lead, zinc, cadmium, gold, and silver—in Kosovo. As a result, U.S.-led NATO war planes evoked images of Tokyo and Dresden. Saturation bombing from 15,000 feet done in the name of humanitarianism is what you get when you've earned the label of official enemy, not to mention unexploded land mines and clusters bombs and the deadly legacy of depleted uranium.

Because of the Holocaust, it is relevant when discussing the legacy of WWII to consider the role Israel plays in the post-war world. Can the Jewish state salvage the image of a good war?

It was standard U.S. policy in the years following Germany's surrender to whitewash the records of certain Nazis deemed useful in the never-ending war against communism. Those war criminals, like Klaus Barbie, whose notoriety made such a makeover impossible often ended up in U.S. client states in Latin America. Since this relationship is often too violent for American public consumption, a willing surrogate is needed.

"The Israelis may be seen as American proxies in Honduras and Guatemala," stated Israeli journalist, Yoav Karni in *Yediot Ahronot*. Also, *Ha'aretz* correspondent Gidon Samet has explained that the most important features of the U.S.-Israeli strategic cooperation in the 1980s were not in the Middle East, but with Central America. "The U.S. needs Israel in Africa and Latin America, among other reasons, because of the government's difficulties in obtaining congressional authorization for its ambitious aid programs and naturally, for military actions," Gamet wrote on November 6, 1983, adding that America has "long been interested in using Israel as a pipeline for military and other aid" to Central America.

Earlier that same year, Yosef Priel reported in *Davar* that "Latin America has become the leading market for Israeli arms exports."

Who are these governments so willingly snapping up weapons manufactured in the Holy Land? One illustrative example is Guatemala. In 1981, shortly after Israel agreed to provide military aid to this oppressive regime, a Guatemalan officer had a feature article published in the army's Staff College review. In that article, the officer praised Adolf Hitler, National Socialism, and the Final Solution—quoting extensively from *Mein Kampf* and chalking up Hitler's anti-Semitism to the "discovery" that communism was part of a "Jewish conspiracy." Despite such seemingly incompatible ideology, Israel's estimated military assistance to Guatemala in 1982 was $90 million.[16]

What type of policies did the Guatemalan government pursue with the help they received from a nation populated with thousands of Holocaust survivors? Consider the words of Gabriel, one of the freedom fighters interviewed in 1994 by Jennifer Harbury:

In my country child malnutrition is close to 85 percent. Ten percent of all children will be dead before the age of five, and this is only the number actually reported to government agencies. Close to 70 percent of our people are functionally illiterate. There is almost no industry in our country—you need land to survive. Less than 3 percent of our landowners own over 65 percent of our lands. In the last fifteen years or so, there have been over 150,000 political murders and disappearances.... Don't talk to me about Gandhi; he wouldn't have survived a week here.[17]

Similar stories can be culled from countries throughout the region, but apparently have had no effect on the rulers of the Jewish state. For example, when Israel faced an international arms embargo after the 1967 war, a plan to divert Belgian and Swiss arms to the Holy Land was implemented. These weapons were supposedly destined for Bolivia where they would be transported by a company managed by Klaus Barbie. As in "The Butcher of Lyon."[18]

Any moral reservations of such an arrangement are dismissed with a vague "national security" excuse that should sound familiar to any American. "The welfare of our people and the state supersedes all other considerations," pronounced Michael Schur, director of *Ta'as*, the Israeli state military industry in the August 23, 1983 *Ha'aretz*. "If the state has decided in favor of export, my conscience is clear."

One Jewish figure who might be expected to find fault with such policy is Elie Wiesel. Here is an episode from mid-1985, documented by Yoav Karni in *Ha'aretz*, that should put to rest any exalted expectations of the revered moralist:

When Wiesel received a letter from a Nobel Prize laureate documenting Israel's contributions to the atrocities in Guatemala, suggesting that he use his considerable influence to put a stop to Israel's practice of arming neo-Nazis, Wiesel "sighed" and admitted to Karni that he did not reply to that particular letter.

"I usually answer at once," he explained, "but what can I answer to him?"

One is left to only wonder how Wiesel's silent sigh might have been received if it was in response to a letter not about Jewish complicity in the murder of Guatemalans but instead about the function of Auschwitz in 1943.

✪

Moving to Asia, the after-effects of WWII and the ensuing escalation of the Cold War are still being felt. There is much to learn from the example of China.

As mentioned earlier, immediately after the war's end, the U.S. utilized captured Japanese soldiers in the war against Mao Tsetung's communists—once again demonstrating who the "real" enemy was.

Once *der Führer* was disposed of, all attention was trained back on the real enemy. Fifty thousand U.S. Marines were sent by Truman to Peking to prevent the fall of that city to Mao's guerrillas while America aided in the transport of almost half a million Chinese Nationalist troops to key centers and ports. By 1946, there were 100,000 U.S. military advisors in China and, by 1949, aid to Chiang kai-Shek's Nationalists had reached $3 billion in cash and military supplies—all in the name of enforcing the Truman Doctrine's pledge against "subjugation by armed minorities or outside pressures."

Regardless, Mao's army had the support of the people and eventually gained control of mainland China. Chiang had to retreat to Taiwan (Formosa, at the time) where his men had "prepared their entry two years earlier by terrorizing the islanders into submission—a massacre which took the lives of as many as 28,000 people," says Blum. The CIA was forced to regroup the Nationalists in Burma where the "Chinats," as they were called, engaged in numerous raids into "Chicom" territory right up until 1961. In the meantime, Mao was busy dealing with two wars on his borders (Korea and Vietnam)—and the task of annexing Tibet.

Despite the high level of outrage being voiced recently, the murderous Chinese assault on Tibet elicited little reaction from America when it first began. An official government document at the time declared that the U.S. "has at no time raised a question" regarding China's claims that Tibet was part of Chinese territory.[19] But once Tibet had fallen and the Dalai Lama forced to flee, the CIA saw a golden opportunity to enlist some spiritual assistance in the battle to smash communism—a fact that's been suspiciously missing from the celebrity pleas for awareness.

In a January 25, 1997 Chicago *Tribune* report entitled "The CIA's secret war in Tibet," with rare candor, declared that, "Little about the CIA's skullduggery in the Himalayas is a real secret anymore except maybe to the U.S. taxpayers who bankrolled it," including the entertainment world's financial elite. However, obscured by the media hype is the reality that, before the Chinese onslaught, the Dalai Lama ruled over a harsh feudal serfdom with the proverbial iron fist. As reported by Gary Wilson, "While most of the population lived in extreme poverty, the Dalai Lama lived richly in the 1000-room, 14-story Potala Palace." Even the popular holy man himself admits to owning slaves during his reign, says Wilson.[20]

In 1959, when the Dalai Lama packed up his riches and scurried into exile in neighboring India, the CIA set up and trained an army of Tibetan *contras*. According to the *Chicago Tribune*, potential recruits were asked only one, rather un-Zen-like question by Air Force pilots working with the CIA: "Do you want to kill Chinese?" The guerrillas were actually trained on U.S. soil—in Colorado—and then airdropped into Tibet by "American pilots who would later carry out operations in Laos and Cambodia during the Vietnam War."

The *New York Times* caught wind of the operation in 1961, but sat on the story at the request of the Pentagon.[21]

So, how have the Dalai Lama and his followers been able to maintain world sympathy for four decades? Jamyang Norbu, a leading Tibetan intellectual, told the *Chicago Tribune*:

> For years, the only way Tibetans could get a hearing in the world's capitals was to emphasize our spirituality and helplessness. Tibetans who pick up rifles don't fit into the romantic image we've built up in the Westerner's heads.

And, if one were to judge by what R.E.M.'s lead singer Michael Stipe said in the February 11, 1997 *New York Post*, the strategy works: "[The Tibetans have] done it peacefully without raising swords," the rock star pontificated. "No matter what hardship these people were under, they would not raise a hand against the enemy."

Gary Wilson lends a little perspective. "The prevalence of anti-communism as a near religion in the United States has made it easy to sell slave masters as humanitarians," he states. "The Dalai Lama is not much different from the former slave owners of the Confederate South."[22]

While the *Chicago Tribune* claims that the U.S. government's support for Tibet's pious contras ended in the 1970s, former CIA agent Ralph McGehee says that the Agency "is a prime mover behind the new 1990s campaign promoting the cause of the Dalai Lama and Tibetan independence." McGehee cites the Dalai Lama's eldest brother, a businessman named Gyalo Thondup, as the key player in the new operation.[23]

Apparently, even His Holiness must operate without the luxury of altruism.

While the Soviet Union's sordid role in the "Good War" legacy has been well-documented elsewhere, a full disclosure of Truman Doctrine trauma cannot be found anywhere in the mainstream media. Across the globe, hundreds of millions have suffered under the predatory corporatism and paranoid anti-communism that has defined the much-ballyhooed American century but, as political pundits are inclined to remind us, there are definitely some wayward chickens long overdue in their trip home to roost.

"During the 1980s and early 1990s, the United States seemingly won every war it waged," write John Stauber and Sheldon Rampton, "...[but] while U.S. planners remain obsessed with images and oblivious to the real human needs of the poor, Latin America and the rest of the Third World will remain a hotbed of revolutionary ferment, fueled by the desperation of people for whom dying in battle appears preferable to dying of hunger. In a very real sense, the Third World War has already begun—but thanks to clever public relations, it simply hasn't been announced."[24]

Like WWII and the Cold War, there is nothing inevitable about this unannounced Third World War. Whether or not we continue the cycle of devastating military interventions and economic warfare depends upon human decision-making. History is neither a force of nature nor part of some pre-ordained geo-political theory. Certain decisions have been consistently made in the past; we each can play a role in making sure different choices are made from now on.

Recognizing the lies and deceit that mask the neo-colonial motivations of the U.S. military machine and its corporate sponsors is a giant first step towards attaining the type of international awareness and solidarity needed to avoid further global conflict. To take that step, however, first requires the rejection of myth-making and denial.

MYTH AMERICA

Mythology, for most Americans, evokes images of Jupiter, Hercules, and Thor; it's something the primitive ancients engaged in before modernity reared its enlightened head. But the United States is a nation built upon a foundation of myth and there are many forms of mythology that have taken hold since WWII: free markets, Western supremacy, the cult of science and technology, fundamentalist demagoguery—to name a few. Such deeply-held tenets could only become acceptable in a society consciously and purposefully conditioned to worship wealth, consumerism, and the unquestioned preservation of power at any cost. But, it is through independent thought and serious inquiry that the myriad cracks in this rickety facade are duly exposed.

The "Good War" fable endures—despite the fact that "the adjective and the noun don't match"[25]—because it caters to a basic need to recast our actions and the actions of those we are taught to revere in a new light in order to make it easier to live with these actions and still maintain a positive self-image. If the working class is kept unaware of what is being done in their name, rebellion is unlikely. If the average citizen in inundated with images designed to demonstrate that the U.S. government has always acted in a benevolent manner, rebellion appears unnecessary. As a result, justification is crucial and common for those in power and the masses they need to manipulate into denial.

Films like Steven Spielberg's *Saving Private Ryan* are popular attempts at such justification. Even if war is hell and the good guys sometimes lose their way, these vehicles teach us that there is still no reason to question the morality of the mission or the stature of that particular generation.

More pointedly, Tom Brokaw's bestselling book, *The Greatest Generation,* informs those who came of age during the era of Reagan and Rambo that those who came of age during the Depression and WWII were indeed "the greatest generation any society has ever produced." This was a generation that would takes its rightful place alongside those "who had converted the North American wilderness into the United States," Brokaw declares without a hint of irony. Such patriotic prose, offered up within a receptive climate of post-Cold War insolence, enables the NBC news anchor to proclaim that "America's preeminent physicists were in a secret race to build a new bomb before Germany figured out how to harness the atom as a weapon,"[27] without worrying about messy details like the Nazis giving up on the bomb well before any "secret race" could commence.

More than just a good war, Brokaw sees WWII as "the greatest war the world has seen," and the GIs who fought in it did so against "great odds, but they did not protest" (this despite 43,000 conscientious objectors and a total of 350,000 cases of draft evasion[27]). Thus, thanks to the seductive power of myth, millionaire celebrities like Brokaw, Spielberg, and many others gain further wealth and prestige by playing the role of corporate/military propagandist to an audience deceived and pacified by jingoistic hysteria and the solace it often provides.

Much of this is possible because the "Good War" myth granted the U.S. the freedom to intervene practically at will across the globe. After all, who could question Uncle Sam's motives when his boys had just saved the world from Hitler? Upon the end of the Cold War and the defeat of yet another evil empire, the Soviet deterrent essentially vanished. This development provided further latitude for the U.S. to frame its military actions as humanitarian, as part of a democratic new world order forged on the battlefields of WWII and affirmed during the Cold War. America is simply defending freedom, we're told, and who could possibly be against freedom?

Saving Private Ryan and *The Greatest Generation* can only serve to reinforce this form of denial by preying upon a citizenry wishing to believe the best about its country. Such books, films, and other forms of pop culture help provide cover for the rich and powerful who seek global dominion through imperialism and warfare while simultaneously keeping much of the general public fragmented and uninformed about alternatives.

However, those who view such manipulation as inescapable, insurmountable, and perhaps even necessary are yet again ignoring the historical record this time by underestimating the inspirational power of collective human action.

LEARNING FROM THE PAST

Revolutionary pacifist A.J. Muste wondered in 1941, "The problem after war is with the victor. He thinks he has just proved that war and violence pay. Who will now teach him a lesson?"[28] Precisely how and when such a lesson will be taught is not known, but it can safely be assumed that this lesson will never be learned from a standard college textbook, an insipid bestseller, or a box office smash. However, one can hope the conduit for learning will be a shared sense of curiosity and skepticism along with an indomitable desire for solidarity and justice.

Comedian and social commentator Lenny Bruce declared that "Truth comes to all of us at different degrees and levels." It doesn't matter who first discovers and exposes the truth behind a dangerous myth. What is most important is that this truth and the power it carries is shared and further questions are asked.

"To ask serious questions about the nature and behavior of one's own society is often difficult and unpleasant," concludes Noam Chomsky. "Difficult because the answers are generally concealed, and unpleasant because the answers are often not only ugly...but also painful. To understand the truth about these matters is to be led to action that may not be easy to undertake and that may even carry significant personal cost."[29]

Some serious questions have been posed herein and the few answers provided were often ugly and painful. What remains unknown is whether or not these answers will lead to action despite the "significant personal cost" such action may entail. One thing is certain, however: without such organizing, action, and sacrifice, there will be many more wars—both good and bad—and many more lies told to obscure the truth about them.

NOTES FOR CHAPTER EIGHT

1. Chomsky, *Tide*, p. 118
2. Stauber and Rampton, p. 197
3. Chomsky, *Tide*, p. 57
4. Zinn, p. 417
5. Blum, Hope, p. 35
6. Zinn, p. 418
7. Blum, *Hope*, p. 216
8. Blum, p.216
9. Blum p. 220
10. Diana Johnstone. "Seeing Yugoslavia Through the Dark Glass: Politics, Media, and the Ideology of Globalization," *Covert Action Quarterly* Fall 1998, p. 9.
11. Johnstone, p. 11
12. Johnstone, p. 12
13. Johnstone, p. 12
14. Sara Flounders. *Bosnia Tragedy: The Unknown Role of the U.S. Government & Pentagon* (New York: World View Forum, 1995) p. 2
15. Thomas Deichman "Misinformation: TV Coverage of the Bosnian Camp," *Covert Action Quarterly* Fall 1998, p. 52
16. Excerpts from Israeli press quote by Chomsky in Tide, p. 34-6
17. Jennifer Harbury. *Bridge of Courage: Life Stories of the Guatemalan Comañeros and Compañeras* (Monroe, ME: Common Courage Press, 1994), p. 78
18. Chomsky, *Tide*, p. 36. Despite such behavior in Latin America, Israel's role as a Middle East enforcer is far more important to U.S. economic/military policy. A quick overview is offered here by Kenneth C. Davis (p. 406): "On a simplistic American scale of good versus bad, Israel [is] democratic and pro-western. Over the years, a pro-Israel lobby, organized for maximum voting impact, kept Israel well armed and well supported. Strategically, Israel [is] a reliable client-state in the midst of unstable Arab lands." For a more detailed analysis of Israel's role in U.S. foreign policy, read the updated edition of *Fateful Triangle: The United States, Israel & The Palestinians*, by Noam Chomsky (Boston: South End Press, 1999)
19. Blum, Hope, p. 23
20. Gary Wilson discussed the *Chicago Tribune* revelations in the Feb. 6, 1997 issue of *Workers World*.
21. Blum, *Hope*, p. 26

22. Wilson, *Workers World*

23. Wilson, *Workers World*. This discussion of the Dalai Lama and Tibet is not meant to downplay Chinese atrocities or ignore the importance of the struggle for self-determination. Rather, the Tibet issue is offered here as a prime example of the cynical manipulation of the masses by the capitalist elite and corporate media.

24. Stauber and Rampton, p. 178

25. Studs Terkel, quoted by Harvey, p. 12

26. Tom Brokaw. *The Greatest Generation* (New York: Random House, 1998), pp. xxx, 11, xix. (Brokaw is a news anchor for NBC-TV which is owned by General Electric, a major defense industry contractor.) It is worth considering whether or not Brokaw's book (or Spielberg's movie) would have been so readily embraced before, say, the 1980s. Those who came of age in the Reagan/Bush era, when the military enjoyed a comeback of sorts in the world of pop culture and new technologies beamed that message further and faster than ever before, appear to be a more receptive audience for such myth-building.

27. Zinn, p. 409

28. Zinn, p. 416

29. David Cogswell. *Chomsky for Beginners* (New York: Readers and Writers Publishing, Inc., 1996) p. 135

BIBLIOGRAPHY

Adams, Michael C.C. *The Best War Ever: America and World War II* (Baltimore and London: The Johns Hopkins University Press, 1994)

Agel, Jerome and Glanze, Walter D. *Cleopatra's Nose, The Twinkie Defense, & 1500 Other Verbal Shortcuts in Popular Parlance* (New York: Prentice Hall Press, 1990)

Alperovitz, Gar. *The Decision to Use the Atomic Bomb and the Architecture of an American Myth* (New York: A. A. Knopf, 1995)

Ambrose, Stephen E. *Citizen Soldiers: The U.S. Army from the Normandy Beaches to the Bulge to the Surrender of Germany, June 7, 1944 to May 7, 1945* (New York: Touchstone, 1997)

Antonine, Chet. "Johnny Sold His Gun: The Untold Story of U.S. Outlaw GIs in WWII Europe," *Loompanics Main Catalog*, 1992: 1-6

Bacque, James. *Other Losses: The Shocking Truth*

Behind the Mass Deaths of Disarmed German Soldiers and Civilians Under General Eisenhower's Command (Rocklin, CA: Prima Publishing, 1991)

Barksy, Robert F. *Noam Chomsky: A Life of Dissent* (Cambridge, MA: The MIT Press, 1997)

Bird, William L., Jr. and Rubenstein, Harry R. *Design for Victory: World War II Posters on the American Home Front* (New York: Princeton Architectural Press, 1998)

Blum, William. *Killing Hope: U.S. Military and CIA Interventions Since World War II* (Monroe, ME: Common Courage Press, 1995)
—. "Hiroshima: Needless Slaughter, Useful Terror," *Covert Action Quarterly*, Summer 1995: 22-25

Bullock, Alan. *Hitler and Stalin: Parallel Lives* (New York: Vintage, 1991, 1993)

Caldicott, Helen. *Nuclear Madness: What You Can Do* (New York: W.W. Norton and Company, 1978, 1994)

Carnes, Mark C., ed. *Past Imperfect: History According to the Movies* (New York: Henry Holt and Company, 1995)

Chomsky, Noam. "History and Memory," interviewed by David Barsamian, audiocassette, *Alternative Radio*, 1995
—. *Chronicles of Dissent: Interviews with David Barsamian* (Monroe, ME: Common Courage Press, 1992)
—. *What Uncle Sam Really Wants* (Berkeley, CA: Odonian Press, 1992)
—. *The Chomsky Reader* (James Peck, editor) (New York: Pantheon Books, 1987)

—. *Turning the Tide: US Intervention in Central America and the Struggle for Peace* (Boston: South End Press, 1985)

Churchill, Ward. "Assaults on Truth and Memory, Part I," *Z Magazine* December 1996: 31-37

—. "Assaults on Truth and Memory, Part II," *Z Magazine* February 1997: 42-47.
—. "Fascism, the FBI, and Native Americans," interviewed by David Barsamian, audiocassette, *Alternative Radio*, 1995

Clark, Ramsey. *The Fire This Time: U.S. War Crimes in the Gulf* (New York: Thunder's Mouth Press, 1992)

Cockburn, Alexander. *The Golden Age Is In Us: Journeys & Encounters* (London: Verso, 1995)

Cogswell, David. *Chomsky for Beginners* (New York: Writers and Readers, 1996)

Cole, Wayne S. *Charles A. Lindbergh and the Battle Against American Intervention in World War II* (New York: Harcourt Brace Jovanovich, 1974)

Davis, Daniel S. *Behind Barbed Wire: The Imprisonment of Japanese Americans During World War II* (New York: E. P. Dutton, 1967)

Davis, Kenneth C. *Don't Know Much About History: Everything You Need to Know about American History but Never Learned* (New York: Avon Books, 1990)

Deichman, Thomas. "Misinformation: TV Coverage of the Bosnian Camp," *Covert Action Quarterly* Fall 1998: 52-55

Doares, Bill. "Corporate America & the Rise of Hitler," *Workers World* May 4, 1995: 11

Dower, John W. *War Without Mercy: Race & Power in the Pacific War* (New York, Pantheon Books, 1986)

Downey, John. "*LOOT* Interviews Carole Gallagher," *Lies of Our Times*, April 1994: 14-18

Eckardt, Steve. "Global Extermination: Neither Fire Nor Water This Time," *Third World Resurgence*, #51: 4-6

Edoin, Hoito. *The Night Tokyo Burned* (New York: St. Martin's Press, 1987)

Feingold, Henry L. *The Politics of Rescue: The Roosevelt Administration and the Holocaust, 1938-1945* (New Brunswick, NJ: Rutgers University Press, 1970)

Finkelstein, Norman G. *Image and Reality in the Israel-Palestine Conflict* (New York: Verso, 1995, 1997)

Flounders, Sara. *Bosnia Tragedy: The Unknown Role of the U.S. Government & Pentagon* (New York: World View Forum, 1995)

Fussell, Paul. *Wartime: Understanding and Behavior in the Second World War* (New York: Oxford University Press, 1989)

Gagnon, Bruce. *Cassini Fact Sheet, Florida Coalition for Peace & Justice*, 1996

Galeano, Eduardo. *Open Veins of Latin America: Five Centuries of the Pillage of a Continent* (New York, Monthly Review Press, 1973, 1997)

Grossman, Karl. "Nukes in Space," interviewed by David Barsamian, audiocassette, *Alternative Radio,* 1996

Hatfield, J.H. *Fortunate Son: George W. Bush and the Making of an American President* (New York, NY: Soft Skull Press, 2000)

Hallock, Daniel William. *Hell, Healing and Resistance: Veterans Speak* (Farmington, PA: The Plough Publishing House, 1998)

Harbury, Jennifer. *Bridge of Courage: Life Stories of the Guatemalan Compañeros and Compañeras* (Monroe, ME: Common Courage Press, 1994)

Harvey, Miles. "Remembering the Good War: Interview with Studs Terkel," *In These Times,* August 7, 1995: 12-16

Herman, Edward S. *Beyond Hypocrisy: Decoding the News in the Age of Propaganda* (Boston: South End Press, 1992)

Herzstein, Robert Edwin. *Roosevelt and Hitler: Prelude to War* (New York: Paragon House, 1989)

Higham, Charles. *Trading with the Enemy: The Nazi-American Money Plot,* 1933-1949 (New York: Barnes & Noble Books, 1983)

International Action Center. *Metal of Dishonor, Depleted Uranium: How the Pentagon Radiates Soldiers and Civilians with DU Weapons* (New York, IAC, 1997)

Jenning, Peter and Brewster, Todd. *The Century* (New York: Doubleday, 1998)

Johnstone, Diana. "Seeing Yugoslavia Through the

Dark Glass: Politics, Media, and the Ideology of Globalization," *Covert Action Quarterly* Fall 1998: 9-19

Kaku, Michio. "Legacy of Nuclear Weapons," interviewed by David Barsamian, audiocassette, *Alternative Radio*, 1995

Kelley, Robin D.G. *Hammer and Hoe: Alabama Communists During the Great Depression* (Chapel Hill: University of North Carolina Press, 1990)

Kennedy, David M. *Freedom from Fear: The American People in the Depression and War, 1929-1945* (New York: Oxford University Press, 1999)

Klehr, Harvey; Haynes, John Earl; and Firsor, Fridrilch Igorevich. *The Secret World of American Communism* (New Haven: Yale University Press, 1995)

Krammer, Arnold. *Nazi Prisoners of War in America* (Lanham, MD: Scarborough House, 1979, 1991, 1996

Lacey, Robert. *Little Man: Meyer Lansky and the Gangster Life* (Boston: Little, Brown and Company, 1991)

Lifton, Robert Jay and Mitchell, Greg. *Hiroshima in America: Fifty Years of Denial* (New York: Grosset/Putnam, 1995)

Lookstein, Haskel. *Were We Our Brothers' Keepers? The Public Response of American Jews to the Holocaust 1938-1944* (New York: St. Martin's Press, 1987)

Lyttle, Richard B. *Il Duce: The Rise and Fall of Benito Mussolini* (New York: Antheum, 1987)

Mee, Charles L. *Meeting at Potsdam* (New York: M. Evans, 1975)

McKee, Alexander. Dresden 1945: *The Devil's Tinderbox* (New York: Dutton, 1984)

Montague, Peter. "Experiments: Radiation Then, Chemicals Now," *Lies of Our Times*, April 1994: 12-13

Morse, Arthur D. *While Six Million Died: A Chronicle of American Apathy* (Woodstock, NY: The Overlook Press, 1967)

New York Daily News, reprint of August 15, 1945 edition

Null, Gary. *The '90s Healthy Body Book: How to Overcome the Effects of Pollution and Cleanse the Toxins from Your Body* (Deerfield Beach, FL: Health Communications, Inc., 1994)

Parenti, Michael. *Blackshirts & Reds: Rational Fascism and the Overthrow of Communism* (San Francisco: City Lights, 1997)

Perry, Marvin. *Western Civilization: A Brief History, Volume II, From the 1400s* (Boston: Houghton Mifflin, 1997)

Polmar, Norman and Allen, Thomas B. *World War II: The Encyclopedia of the War Years, 1941-1945* (New York: Random House, 1996)

Pool, James and Suzanne. *Who Financed Hitler?: The Secret Funding of Hitler's Rise to Power, 1919-1933* (New York: Dial Press, 1978)

Prange, Gordon William. *At Dawn We Slept: The Untold Story of Pearl Harbor* (New York: Viking,

1991)

Preston, William Jr. "Our Friend the Atom," *Lies of Our Times*, Jan.-Feb. 1994: 23-25

Raico, Ralph. *World War I*, audiocassette, Carmichael, 1989

Robbins, John. *Reclaiming Our Health: Exploding the Medical Myth and Embracing the Source of True Healing* (Tiburon, CA: HJ Kramer, 1996)

Rosenbaum, Ron. "Hitler and the Poison Kitchen," *George*, July 1998: 68-71, 108

Shalom, Stephen R. "V-J Day: Remembering the Pacific War," *Z Magazine* July/August 1995: 71-82

Shenkman, Richard. *Legends, Lies & Cherished Myths of World History* (New York: HarperPerennial, 1994)

Simpson, Christopher. *Blowback: America's Recruitment of Nazis and its Effect on the Cold War* (New York: Weidenfeld & Nicolson, 1988)

Spiegelman, Bob. "*LOOT* Interviews Christopher Simpson," *Lies of Our Times* May 1994: 13-18.

Spula, Jack Bradigan. "The Untold Story of Nuclear Experiments," *Lies of Our Times*, April 1994: 10-11

Stauber, John and Rampton, Sheldon. *Toxic Sludge is Good for You! Lies, Damn Lies and the Public Relations Industry* (Monroe, ME: Common Courage Press, 1995)

Stone, I.F. *The War Years, 1939-1945* (Boston: Little Brown and Company, 1988)

Stromberg, Joseph. *World War II*, audiocassette,

Carmichael, 1989

Takaki, Ronald. *Hiroshima: Why America Dropped the Atomic Bomb* (Boston: Little, Brown and Company, 1995)

Taylor, Fred, ed. *The Goebbels Diaries, 1939-1941* (London: H. Hamilton, 1982)

Udall, Stewart. *Myths of August* (New York: Pantheon Books, 1994)

Vankin, Jonathan. *Conspiracies, Cover-ups and Crimes: Political Manipulation and Mind Control in America* (New York: Paragon House Publishers, 1992)

Watkins, T.H. *The Great Depression: America in the 1930s* (Boston: Little, Brown and Company, 1993)

Weitz, John. *Hitler's Banker: Hjalmar Horace Greeley Schacht* (Boston: Little Brown and Company, 1997)

Wittner, Lawrence S. *Rebels Against War: The American Peace Movement, 1933-1983* (Philadephia: Temple University Press, 1984)

World Almanac and Book of Facts (Mahwah, NJ: World Almanac Books, 1999)

Wright, David K. *A Multicultural Portrait of World War II* (New York: Marshall Cavendish, 1994)

Wright, Mike *What They Didn't Teach You About World War II* (Novato, CA: Presidio Press, 1998)

Wyman, David S. *The Abandonment of the Jews: America and the Holocaust, 1941-1945* (New York: Pantheon Books, 1984)

Yancey, Diane *Life in a Japanese-American Internment Camp* (San Diego: Lucent Books, 1998)

Zepezauer, Mark. *The CIA's Greatest Hits* (Tucson, AZ: Odonian Press, 1994)

Zinn, Howard. *A People's History of the United States, 1492-Present* (New York: HarperPerennial, 1980, 1995)

INDEX